Golden Handcuffs Review

Golden Handcuffs Review Publications

Seattle, Washington

Golden Handcuffs Review Publications

Editor

Lou Rowan

Contributing Editors

Andrea Augé
Stacey Levine
Rick Moody
Toby Olson
Jerome Rothenberg
Scott Thurston
Carol Watts

Guiding Intelligence

David Antin

LAYOUT MANAGEMENT BY PURE ENERGY PUBLISHING, SEATTLE
WWW.PUREENERGYPUB.COM

Libraries: *this is Volume II, #25.*

Information about subscriptions, donations, advertising at:
www.goldenhandcuffsreview.com

Or write to: Editor, Golden Handcuffs Review Publications
1825 NE 58th Street, Seattle, WA 98105-2440

Contents

RESPONSE

from *Mice 1961, a novel*

Stacey Levine

The story of the two sisters was minted when the world's air was fresh. Many versions exist. In some, the events are barbed and hot, confused as life really is. The siblings struggle. In one variation, the two argue and fight beside a mill's cold stream. The younger one falls and drowns, but once dead, grows wings. In another version, the dead one transforms into a harp who sings.

Some follow widely-venerated plot patterns. Some stories reveal themselves mildly and weakheartedly in the face of life; some emphasize the sisters' beautifully curious, humid faces and young, swaying gaits. Other versions portray the girls as otherworldly, and the sound of their speech so striking it resounds in other stories nearby. One variation has it that the girls part in blinding rain, reuniting only after many adventures that, though invented, are true.

Some stories are dense as pudding with a set skin, no further words possible to add, none to omit.

It could start with an immediate climax in which those in power are held down and stabbed.

So many stories sprint callowly to perfunctory and false endings, tidy, uplifting, and untrue.

If told through a different lens, would it fall apart?

Often, one sister becomes more prominent in the plot, resembling other centrally figured girls, like the weakish-type movie-star: she's blonde. Girdled inside a film's frames or candied for TV, she is nervous and ever-alert, for the plot watches her obsessively, as if through a microscope. Her appetite is not for herself. She isn't hearty and has no overbite or lisp; she can't wear bulky oxford shoes.

Why, anyway, did the older sister force Mice to wear those awful, clumsy, brad-covered shoes?

A story should set out to convince the listener there's no other way.

Perhaps it's best to tell my version of Mice in a long, clenched series of asides.

Although to describe is to contaminate, I began my try.

*****

Face it, Mice's eyes were simply not right.

Neighbors said her out-of-date blouses, oaf shoes, and the bottomless absence of tint in her skin made her a shadow in reverse—a white elephant or a ghost, they said. Those weak, wobbly eyes were the worst.

Her startling-white appearance, the result of a one-in-twenty thousand chromosomal disorder, had been a lifelong disaster for the sisters' mother Candy, who'd endured the girl's growing-up years mostly in bed, full of shame.

Now Candy was gone and Mice scuttled along the sidewalks every evening. After being cooped up through the days, it must've been a release. Neighbors gathered routinely at Parrott's Grocery near 74th or in front of Gorge Discount to watch.

Some felt sorry for running Mice, with her excessive whiteness. They wondered aloud: Is that longish white down on her limbs a sign that her life is hard, or that all of life is? Had the down emerged because of Candy? As she sped past the porch-lounging neighbors near sunset, they pointed out her tiny teeth and forehead spattered with pinprick freckles, taking care to note that Mice, whenever she coughed, turned both scarlet and blue.

"Those eyebrows!" they remarked as she passed.

At times, neighbors spoke my most atrocious thoughts so precisely.

They said the girl's thick frost eyebrows turned their stomachs; they took offense at her fuzzy, half-airborne, colorless hair, complaining that Mice ruined the neighborhood with her head and body, blinding everyone with her terrible all-whiteness to boot.

Face it, even if her older, longsuffering sister Jody had coiffed, straightened, and treated the younger girl's awful, marled-yellowish undertracts of hair and dressed her in silky sleeveless blouses, too, neighbors would've disapproved.

And face it, some neighbors maligned Mice for not being pristinely white enough, complaining that her shade, that of dullish sour cream, should be brighter.

The milkscape of the girl's neck and shoulders made them lazy and liable to shout uncontrolled remarks, they said. From the porch at Parrotts, they spoke routinely against those indistinct, twitching eyes that couldn't even function in bright sun, and they grew irate over the paintbrush-like eyelashes, too, not to mention the lashes' jarring cream-orange tips, which, whenever the girl removed her oversized sunglasses, threw neighbors into rages.

Waking and congregating earlier every day, neighbors, it seemed, had a thirst, either for the girl or for dismissing her; wasn't it so unlucky, they said, that Mice'd been born as she was and with such poor luck besides, only to be larded with problems nobody ever had heard of or understood? In addition, the language lacked words to describe Mice thoroughly.

Once, I heard Al Parrott tell the morning clutch of neighbor-customers on the porch that Mice's growing-up problems eventually had worsened to completely obscure her sight in the way seeping oil slowly ruins good wood. Other neighbors, fully confined to their points of view, told various stories of Mice while explaining that, for them, the merest mention of the girl sent immediate thrills of gratitude through them for whatever degree of vision they actually possessed.

So, because of Mice, neighbors grew more sure of themselves. They slept better each night.

Watching her speeding furtively at dusk past the storefronts' ruby bricks, riling up the dust up so it coated her hands and arms, or spying her while she sat on the apartment stairs at night without even a handkerchief beneath her and furiously stripping down radios, they complained that Mice was too tiny or large, or simply bothersome with her padded hands and outer ears so peel-thin and devoid of the folds that normally characterize others' ear-tops. Neighbors also disliked Mice, they said, because of her habit of asking abrupt, off-topic questions, not to mention the fact that her eyes were small and blue, twitching under duress and at most other times, too.

They couldn't agree, either, as to what Mice actually looked like or what she was doing on Reef Way. Some thought she could see fairly well at close range, but not across any distance; others said her eyes were overall adequate but her biggest defects were her offputting all-whiteness, animal laziness, and selfishness. Some swore she was stone blind, and in the end, no one really knew what Mice could or couldn't see.

*****

As I lay in my place behind the lint-colored sofa, I studied her often as she sat emptily at her hobby table, touching her wooden boxes of radio parts, the peppery freckles across her nose and cheeks a little mask of runes that made me wonder: Are patterns, by the fact of their existence, asking to be observed and deciphered, or do they just blindly occur?

What color were Mice's small, flat hands anyway? Strawberry-pink.

Four Poems

Rae Armantrout

NEW DEVELOPMENTS

Pine trunks touched
by the same wind
almost feel it.

*

We invented sex
and violence

because our systems
needed content,

something to deliver,

something that could cross
the gaps.

*

You think I have that backwards?

*

We press spine to spine
and our captive
glow-worms chatter.

What do you think they're
going on about?

*

When we were simpler,
we spoke with others.

"Are you there?" we asked
cell to cell.

Now we're mostly
talking to ourselves.

GRASP

Is it fair to say

you want the scene described

in as much detail

as possible

as if it were a place

where you could be found

and rescued?

*

The homeless banter at tables
set out by the supermarket Starbucks.

"Everybody Wants to Rule the World"
drifts from the store's sound system.

One woman sleeps stubbornly
upright –
cradled in her arm,
a bottle of 7-Up.

*

If to recognize
is to watch yourself

grasp

UNDERWRITING

A takes advantage
of her opportunities.
By that I mean
she knows which
of her neighbors
is volatile
and prone to decompose.

*

In D's version,
the music teacher is important
only because he appears
"mysteriously"
to give D four lessons

before killing himself.

*

For E,
each crisp leaf
is "another leaf"

until heaven
is hell.

*

Heaven/hell is
an infinite number
of universes
in each of which
the creator underwrites
one of his creatures'
delusions
until belief -
or patience - wavers
and a collapse begins.

*

A "lives"
by reacting
B with C
and evanescing D
as waste

FRAME

Why are the bare twigs in the window,
clouds inching between their knuckles,
worth watching?

"Wanting more from the day
is a form
of greed," you said –
or maybe "grief."

Two clouds separate so slowly that, at first, it could be
an illusion. Yet, within minutes, the smaller disappears
beyond the frame's horizon,
leaving no room for doubt.

Bits and Pieces

Rosmarie Waldrop

1.

Bits and pieces, you say, scratching your beard. That's what there is.
Stalks rising in the air as if gravity did not exist. Roots, dirt, turtles,
elephants. Because the singular wastes territory we try to link it
to galaxies or melting ice. For a coherent universe. But not dense
enough to attract, mere pieces, always, just as they were. Is this why
we have offspring? Why I say *my* hand, *my* foot, to make them more
intimately felt than objects usually are in the mind? Can the withness
of the body undo isolation?

2.

This almost physical wanting of continuity, if possible, happiness.
It makes us smooth over the gaps with a twist of muscle on a field
of error. We call it instinct, and it spreads like a heatwave. Even to
the distant mountain whose slopes seem softer for being beyond
touch. But our ambitions contradict one another: you also love this
particular patch of blue in the sky. You fear debris in the brain will
bury this one insistent hydrangea that stands out from the sprawl of

green. You say hydrangea. And again: hydrangea. As if the intensity
of the word could keep the plant in bloom.

3.
If memory serves, it was five years ago that yours began to refuse.
Is it now like crossing from an open field into the woods, the sunlight
suddenly switched off? Or like a roof without edge or frame, pushed
sideways in time? Like the flashes in which we think we possess
though never quite reach ourselves? Yet today is today. And you
receive it, if in pieces. Likewise words. If intermittently. Then you let
them move over your tongue and hold their possible bodies in both
hands.

4.
It seemed almost personal when the sun was eclipsed. As if visibility
were like your memory, or the moon's shadow the cataract on my
eye. Observing the latter did not make it pass. Unlike when a fright
resolves into the joy of not yet. I keep on standing as I've learned
to, having feet. Though electrons degenerate and the knife-edge
is moving closer. I treasure the residues of love's radiation, put on
sneakers and wait for the form of rejection to come. Whether you'll
no longer know my name or walk out of your body, I anticipate I'll
swallow. As if it were a hard object.

5.
Meanwhile you cling to your book. Do the words still float you to
Prospero's island? Or drop, separate coins, bringing no dew from
the Bermudas? I put my hope in the fundamental difference between
local time and time at a distance. Make a show of clearly contoured
identity, no matter if you can connect it to family structure. A stable
body with only occasional modification. Rather than molecules
and feelings in violent agitation. Let alone quanta dissolving into
vibrations of light. You stare at your left little finger, which is crooked.

6.

Veins visible under your skin, translucent. The first stage of a fare-thee-well? Cypress, pine, yew, taxus, the evergreen punctuation of our final sentence? Elsewhere, in territories off the map, does time warp, whirl, meander, fold, get trapped in wormholes? Careen into complexities of curves and lives we will not have? Here, the clocks are synchronized with dusty noise. And breath is short. I count the pulse pushing through my neck and try to match it to your breathing. The escape velocity of the unknown.

7.

Perhaps if we had dark-adapted eyes. The shadows would not overtake us. And you could brush your teeth without fearing for their skin. Add the conjunction of being prudent, and night broader and deeper. Because you are still within it. Could this not disperse the threat? As in a mirror? Could it not offer the possibility that your illness, even if deliberate in its purpose, need not proceed in a straight line? Could slow in the gravitational drag of my body?

8.

Am I trying to write my anxieties down into the deep of the paper? In such a way that I could draw them back inside me? Completely? This has nothing to do with poetry, but perpetuates denial and mental reservations. To my surprise you say that even blind with incomprehension, we must. Trust the words we still have. With their tangled depths and roots. To house the world in the complex of our feeling. As if they could love us.

from *Meridian*

☆

Nancy Gaffield

IV   **Boston to Sand le Mere**
         ORDNANCE SURVEY MAP 261: BOSTON

--The line, like life, has no end.
     Tim Ingold, *Lines*

Highest of alerts
     heaviest of hearts
         in memorium for six dead
         scores injured on Westminster Bridge

--all bright and glittering in the smokeless air[1]

walking again on trails born of mud
     & thought
         in memorium for seven dead
         scores injured on London Bridge

---

[1] "all bright and glittering" William Wordsworth, "Composed upon Westminster Bridge, September 3, 1802)

--London Bridge will NEVER fall down[2]

walking in a landscape of few villages
        centuries of land reclamation
                in memorium for twenty-three dead
                250 injured in Manchester

walking past ghostly control towers & weed-strewn
        remnants of lonely runways
                in memorium for one dead
                ten injured at Finsbury Mosque

walking on what the map calls
        West Fen / Catchwater Drain
                in memorium for Grenfell a lesion of
                flame searing
                        the night sky

in the falling ash
        the dead whisper their names
                with swollen hands I try to catch

we are enmeshed
        with every step my heart is full
            of them

words crawl from the cracks in the clay
        they gather at my feet
            ripe for harvest

the mind unravels along medieval furrow & trough
        spiralling out through
            Lincolnshire

--twilight and evening bell, and after that the dark[3]

---

[2] "London Bridge..." Evening Standard Banner
[3] "twilight and evening bell..." Alfred, Lord Tennyson "Crossing the Bar"

ORDNANCE SURVEY MAP 282 LINCOLNSHIRE WOLDS NORTH
Boston to Louth

In a slow flotilla of ships, they followed John Cotton,
charismatic non-conformist vicar of St Botolph, to the new world.
From every hamlet, village, town

and church. At Bag Endersby the church stands on
greensand, the rock that underpins the chalk hereabouts. Not the
bells that Tennyson heard, but a 13th century font with a pieta that
breaks

your heart. Red arrows and skylark song over Catchwater
Drain. Not a military march but a slow sauntering. Walking the prime
meridian wanting

methylene blue to illumine the invisible world, revealing the
line I walk. When the blackbird sings I whistle, the bird replies, or so
I like to think

some paths are dead ends, others lead to fords and water
too deep to cross. Today the wind blows from the south. Reduced
ceremonial elements. The queen dressed in royal blue, her hat too,
embellished with yellow stars. She delivers her speech. (Next year's
is cancelled). The DUP issue
low-growled threats. Temperatures top 30 for the fifth
consecutive day. Another summer solstice and all the politicians
change direction according to the prevailing winds. In politics the
less you care, the better

you do. I catch the scent of salt and fish. Nordsjön, the sea
my mother and grandmother crossed a century ago, urging me
closer

but every time I travel I am contributing to the Sixth Mass
Extinction. Not absorbed for 25,000 years, the greenhouse gases
from my flight. I cause it, knowing this. The catastrophe is already
here. All of us are enmeshed in this.

On mother's birthday I walk the riverine / lacustrine landscape of the Lincolnshire Wolds. Tennyson's beloved Somersby is cloaked in mist. As Helen did, reciting from memory...may there be no moaning at the bar when I put out to sea. We are all enmeshed and

hotter still the following day. Crossing amber waves, Burwell Walk, 189 acres of arable land. Grassland host to bird's-foot trefoil, lady's bedstraw, hay rattle, bracken. Beneath them lies the shadow of ridges and troughs

the open field system of medieval farming. One furlong for each family. Enough to sustain. Now ploughed over for industrial farming...wheat, barley, sugar beets, oil seed rape...80% in the last sixty years.

Pigs stunned by captive bolt pistol, the sickening thud of forceful blows. The object to destroy the cerebrum whilst keeping the heart pumping for exsanguination.

An infestation of blisters and tears slows me to a halt. Mortification of the flesh by ordnance survey map. Horse flies needing a blood meal to lay their eggs attach themselves.

Snipes Dale. Steep chalk escarpment, old plateau grassland and a disused quarry of red chalk rich in fossils. Limestone the remains of fallen animals. Belemnites, brachiopods. Once sea animals, now meadow pipits, lizards, bee orchids, purple saxifrage. A step away

from them. What is a ghost? A phantom crew appearing through the fog? Remembered lines, letters vibrating on paper, a double exposure, a sudden change in temperature, an animal fossilized or an insect trapped

in amber? It was the promise of an end that led me deeper into the interior. The further I walked the more passion the line excited in me. The whole world became luminous and everywhere this luminous world was traversed by lines outlining all objects. The sun drinks me till I am nothing but white light in an empty vessel.

Not a three-dimensional enclosed entity, but the impression of something that used to be there. Not the line

but the space between.

Louth to Fulstow

Walking the line
field upon field
of grain swirls,
indentations
where animals
slept last night

the trail branches
& tangles through

over-ripe wheat
then opens
to pasture & cattle
then further still
through rosettes of broad green
leaves rich in protein
but discarded,
powerless
to resist the sun,
indifferent to the constancy
of the speed of light
the tuber's purple globes
curve above the soil's surface
basking in the glow
of so much sky

as the farms get bigger
I grow smaller
then finally freed
by the space surrounding me
I am nothing
but a tiny speck of blue
in a yellow cornfield
blue the colour of longing
for the sea at the edge
of the horizon,
the back range of the mountains,
the clouds resembling them
When people came
from the old world
to the new
they brought their seeds,
plants, animals, names
failing to embrace
where they were
but gradually learning
the language of the place

gussock, moor-gallop, piner, windin'

I press the line,
a creation of geography & mathematics
marked out for merchants
& military ships,
into the Wolds
extending beyond flatness
into a confluence
of surface & space,
present & past
the walk an articulation
of ground I compel
the line to know things
in real time
bringing memories
from past into present
seeing clearly now what
Larkin saw--*where sky
and Lincolnshire and water meet*

The mind wanders
with voluptuous sadness
the landscapes of memory
& desire
like fragile skin
so easily torn
by a thorn
terra incognita
the maps once called it

but no map reveals
all that there is
I sleep with
my head pointed North
as Clare did
towards the imperishable stars

At the end of the day
I come back indoors to
news of Charlottesville

an act of domestic terrorism
white men with torches
chanting blood and soil
POTUS says they're
"all good people"
I cannot will not fall
into line

In the middle
of an August day
all over America
the sky grows dark
I watch you sleeping
your mouth open
in the shape of a scream
and I think I don't want
to live in this world
anymore something
has shifted
this is just
the beginning

[IV Boston to Sand le Mere is from the final section of *Meridian*, a long
poem based on a 270-mile walk following the footpaths and bridleways
from Sussex to the Humber in eastern England. The complete poem will be
published by Longbarrow Press in January 2019.]

Being Written

Anne Tardos

EVERY PLACE

Every place a foreign land
        quietly happy another world

Previous lives enveloped in previousness, not yet effaced in effacement

Images loop around nothingness
        entangled in the file of life

Le pont d'Avignon only half exists—it's part of the dance

        Unexpected transformations during a lifetime
                when writing and not writing

    i know, the world could be a large black dog
The spider could be on vacation
—it's just like life

Gently budding love affair
        friendly film crew
                rocking chair

Hesitation tango
        semiotic acrobatics
                performed by an exceptionally talented cat

Curious affinity, high-strung friendships, gender-inflected approach to highly
    sensitive skin.

I Am Latency

I am acutely interested in
      drawn to
         the Kindness Machine

What fuels it
      how to use it

It's clearly the most moving and reassuring of all machines

For this to work, I will need a portable apparatus

One with a tiny hard drive
      that can store
         a few Petabytes of data.

            To accommodate that many files

I would need a much faster processor

This would require a massively parallel system where speed and

      flexibility would be paramount

for my high-performance computing
I would also need an *InfiniBand*

     featuring high throughput and low latency.

THE TIME BEING

Not to upset you, but quantum latency, phase transition, and
thermodynamic nonequilibrium
     all point
         to
         the irreversibility of each event

Subject to this devious inexorability
         we fail at every attempt to reverse direction.

Unidirectional doings awaken in the indefinite continuance of existence.

The footprint is decisive, yet the fetus is clueless—for the time being.

Mai 68

Leslie Kaplan

Une fille qui arrive
en courant
essoufflée
elle est en retard
elle arrive
dans le vestiaire
de l'atelier
à l'usine
et elle dit, elle n'arrête pas de répéter
Vous avez entendu
les étudiants
elle rit sans arrêt
elle n'arrête pas de rire
vous avez entendu
à la radio
ce Cohn-Bendit
pour moi c'est ça
la première image de mai 68

pour moi c'est l'espace

comment ça, l'espace ?

l'espace, la sensation de l'espace
l'usine immobile
et l'espace qui s'ouvre
l'espace tout seul
la sensation de l'espace

il y avait des gens partout
des hommes, des femmes
des jeunes, des vieux
des gens qui grimpaient aux grilles
qui entraient dans les ateliers des autres
qui visitaient
qui exploraient des endroits
juste à côté de leur atelier à eux
et qu'ils n'avaient jamais vus
ils découvraient
ils visitaient
ils s'appropriaient

moi je pense à l'espace, je te dis
une sensation physique
le vide
le calme
le silence
à l'intérieur, derrière les fenêtres
les chaînes immobiles, les machines arrêtées
et dehors, dans la cour
le ciel
le grand ciel bleu et blanc, étalé
très beau
des femmes avaient apporté des chaises
dans la cour
elles tricotaient
tu vois ça ?
des femmes assises sur des chaises
en train de tricoter
dans une cour d'usine

sous le grand ciel bleu et blanc
elles tricotaient
elles discutaient

tout le monde parlait sans arrêt
on parlait de tout
de tout
on parlait de la grève, des étudiants
on parlait des revendications
on parlait des barricades
on parlait des salaires
des horaires
des cadences
on parlait de la société

de la société ?

on parlait de l'école, comment apprendre
et quoi
on parlait des enfants
on parlait du travail
si on l'aimait ou pas
on parlait des hommes et des femmes
on parlait du sexe
on parlait des fous
et qui l'était, d'ailleurs
on parlait de la prison
on parlait de la révolution

on parlait du ciel, des nuages
on cherchait les mots
on les essayait
on les posait
avec précaution

on les brandissait, aussi

on les brandissait, parfois
on était devant l'espace

et le temps
mais l'espace et le temps, c'est le cadre
et penser au cadre, c'est penser
on était amené à penser ce que c'est, penser

circuler, plutôt qu'être à sa place
circuler partout
et les mots aussi circulaient
prenaient des drôles de sens

sur un mur, une fois,
j'ai vu quelqu'un écrire, Je n'ai plus peur

moi j'ai vu écrit
J'étais, je suis, je serai

moi j'ai vu
La vie est unique

il y avait une fille qui allait partout
dans toutes les réunions
débraillée, jolie, jolie
et qui portait quatre montres à chaque poignet

une femme qui n'avait jamais rien lu
et qui s'est mise à lire
comme une folle

une militante angoissée angoissée
qui croyait que la révolution
dépendait d'elle

une femme qui poussait son bébé
dans un landau
et qui aurait voulu aller
manifester

une fille de général
qui avait milité contre la guerre en Algérie

contre la guerre du Vietnam
et qui buvait, du blanc, dès le matin
pendant la grève
elle arrête de boire

une jeune psychiatre
qui aimait les fous
elle citait Freud : la normalité
c'est être assez névrosé
pour tenir compte de la réalité
et assez fou
pour vouloir la changer

une fille déchaînée
qui couchait avec tout le monde
tout le monde

des garçons qui balançaient des pavés
ah mais c'était une passion

les filles aussi

les filles aussi

deux filles qui parlaient de leurs parents
jour et nuit

un vieux qui déclamait
à voix haute
dans la cour de l'usine
des tracts
qu'il avait gardés
de 36

des jeunes immigrés
en blouson
manoeuvres, O.S. sur les chaînes
heureux, heureux
ils couraient dans tous les sens

une vieille ouvrière d'origine polonaise
son mari était mort
tombé d'un échafaudage
tous les jours elle venait
et elle apportait des gâteaux

un tourneur, ouvrier qualifié
célibataire, beau garçon
qui se disait dégoûté de la vie
il venait travailler en pantoufles
pendant la grève il mettait tous les jours
son costume du dimanche
et il faisait toutes les gardes
un transistor collé à l'oreille

une jeune femme qui vivait en ménage
avec une autre femme
elle venait à l'usine avec sa copine et sa petite fille
et elles attendaient, toutes les trois, tranquilles

il y avait des étudiants qui parlaient
tellement bien

une fille qui ne pensait qu'à danser
mais qui ne dansait pas
parce qu'il fallait faire la révolution

un garçon qui décidait
tout d'un coup
qu'il ne ferait pas publicitaire
jamais

on faisait du stop
un fils de famille en voiture de sport décapotable
emmenait des jeunes ouvriers
dans leur usine occupée

et la lutte de classes ?

justement, la lutte de classes

les syndicalistes, pas d'accord entre eux
il y en avait un, d'origine italienne
subtil, inquiet, réfléchi
un autre, homme de l'appareil
qui dénigrait tout
les ouvriers le surnommaient « ben quoi »

un ouvrier immigré espagnol
on l'appelait le Cubain
sérieux, il avait lu Marx
il était là jour et nuit
mais il ne laissait pas ses filles
aller aux manifestations

des instituteurs, surexcités
ils passaient dans les usines
ils faisaient une enquête pour leur journal

des agriculteurs, grands, timides
avec des chemises à carreaux et des bottes
ils avaient apporté des pommes de terre
et toute une journée ils étaient restés
à comparer, à discuter

un travailleur immigré, un vieux
il venait d'Algérie
il vous regardait
en souriant, gentil
avec des yeux noirs lumineux
il disait la Frrrance, ah la Frrrance
on voyait ses mains
abîmées, maigres

les contremaîtres voulaient que le travail reprenne
ils se tenaient dans la rue
devant les grilles fermées
avec leurs cravates et leur rage

on leur riait dessus
vengeance, oui
mais ce n'était pas le plus important

tout le monde pensait sans arrêt
tout le monde essayait de penser
c'était extraordinaire
et complètement normal

assis sur une chaise dans une cour d'usine
adossé aux grilles
on se demandait, ah oui, on se demandait

on était très angoissé
mais l'angoisse était un moteur
pas un frein

on se prenait en charge
on ne se sentait plus abandonné
par la société

abandonné ?

oui, abandonné
comme sur une route de banlieue
où il n'y a rien
que des grands immeubles
des poteaux télégraphiques
et des choses et des choses et des choses

pendant les événements
tout le monde discutait
les jeunes avec les vieux
les étudiants avec les ouvriers
les ouvriers sortaient des usines
les étudiants y entraient

pour les femmes
venir la nuit

parler aux hommes
transgression

on quittait sa cage
on refusait la catégorie, la case et le cas
on voulait être autre chose
qu'une fonction de production

l'identité était questionnée

cette vie, cette vie unique
on ne voulait pas
qu'elle soit plate,
aplatie
qu'elle se déroule sur une seule dimension

des étudiants venaient montrer un film
présenter une pièce de théâtre
on voyait que jouer c'est expérimenter
les mots et l'espace
les sentiments et les situations

quelque chose se passe
tout peut arriver
surprise, étonnement, rencontre
les limites reculent
le présent se déploie
le monde est là, dans les détails
il y a de ces moments
rares, exemplaires
où ce qui s'invente dans la société
est aussi large
aussi vrai
que dans l'art.

Four Poems

Roberta Olson

Hats and Other Fungi

That is a very unusual hat, a mushroom?
Red with white spots, it must be poisonous
I once had a guinea pig,
And it looked nothing like your hat
Not really, all it did was bite me
And hide under the couch
On the other hand,
I have never been bitten by a hat
Yes, hats fit much better than guinea pigs
You must favor balaclavas then
I'll bet you like money even more
You can't see the shape of the sun
Until it is gone
When hats lose their shape
We make them into pillows
Maybe, but glass is slowly melting

And music is slowly fading

Maybe a cloud would be a better metaphor

A burst of bright blue flowing

Into the white

Your hat sounds delicious

May I eat your hat?

I am told it looks like a mushroom.

Since

Since the car vanished

Since the carburetor was removed

Since we took a plane instead

Since I threw away your dishes

And your clothes

Ever since we lost the war

Since the river ran dry

Since everyone is angry

Since dawn is useless

Since they stole my last reptile

And my canary flew away

Since the horse was betrayed

Since the storm is already here

Since we forgot to seek shelter

Since everyone wants to leave

Since the leaves are empty and the branches are low

Since there is no way to describe the sublime

Since the sublime is rarely experienced

Since the world is heavy and dark

Since the sublime exists only in silence and dreams

Since the blue man is quiet and the boss is angry

Since the wind always rises

Since the air is pierced by sirens and cars

Since the town lost its face to the moon

Stickily

The interior ruthless gathering space
In random fluctuation
Its meaning has little to do with eyes
Which means it could be music
Would the ghost of music be an apparition?
Or a whisper?
The ghost of music is the deep silence of chairs
How can you sit on silence?
Wood is the ghost of a tree
It lies in the interstices
And then there is no silence at all
But what about the furniture?
This is where the gathering space comes in
A gathering space could be littered with interstices
Or baskets and time
Blows around changing itself
Time is always on time
It is its own illusion
If the chair is never finished, would that represent infinity?
It would represent a large pile of sticks
Authentic sticks, methodical sticks, literal sticks
But never a chair.

Tangled in Triangles

Shadows of birds from simple lines
Sightless, featherless, frozen in repose
Another bird, a bird as I imagine it
Is static, unable to move, heavy wing
Feathers and arthritic stance
Only erasure will free it.

8 o'clock, dark wet night
Dripping ferns, sirens, a fire truck

The light in the house is on
Then off, then on. The twisting limbs
Of a shrub tangled in triangles
In the faint light.
A book, a shoe, a pen
The roar of another jet
home after many days of travel
Horses falling through the sky

The flowers protest
They wait for the right moment
Like medieval archers shooting flaming arrows
Luminous glass of St. Denis blue
It is a hot July night or a morning in March
I feel safe when I'm alone
Yellow on the yellow pillow
Tangled in triangles
Home again after many days travel
Horses falling through the sky

Our lady of errata

Lisa Samuels

the day replays the men on ladders, seeping trees tickling low-hanging clouds, children's feet getting hot in the sun, the swishing strength of the runner in the trapped water flicking the insect's wing as it scrambles off the roof, the last breath of the perishing primate and the first of the new baby; these excrescences we savor with our stories of violence *with even what I have written to you*, not authenticity but a fully inhabited pose needing a real death to achieve it, the shower scene the bath scene the hidden area at the edge of the park — *but what are the means to express, how much has to be there making the strange familiar, your tongue complicit with the writ* in the disputed page, so toned and ruling your internal eye as though seeing were the very last bastion, *yes* the penultimate night having held open the suitcase to receive the meats, me mordi el brazo y exclame, after all as the strange investigates itself your arms hold that event supplanted in a witness, clear shaft dormant in the googled laugh, clear strength dormant in the what-you-nearly parishioned, what you spleen on a wait protected from a violation from outside, where the ordinary feels most real, *your flesh is all the thoughts you believe* you are a kit to add on, volition or desire double the instants you'll perceive, you'll see you're going *in* to the time before all this, before this she was walking next to the median with its lovely machinery of body verdes como una esmeralda, where she is sitting now breathing the syncopation of the letter or intended reader also holding the achieved symbiosis of alterity, *I mean the actual as projection, blinking eyes of a nomadic "you" that came out early in the mind* she is reeling with it, sinks over to the dizzy atrophy of that reel

the screen sinks over the basin, the eyes roll to it, her blood moves ampishly fast as it needs to where the sink is still far away her mind bobs up and down fetching all the warm sloshing near itself and holding the door's look, whose rectangle will support her paroxysms of seeing, eyes upturned toward an idea of who will enter when, the door like an enormous eyelid tilted on its side, the doorknob's point...

and beyond that the hills roll safety through, you penetrate an educated guess about the woman falling, there she is her skirts alive in air, that story of the ceremony you adapt so nothing will flange you right then, if you turn away it isn't real *no one has seen you anyway* the man at the gate is permitted to say nothing that will change what happens (no one sees the cello sheet slip through the casement), someone else you heard inside the washing cellular freshness culture mouths again (and again the tāina) the wet exchange of lobes talking informationally stringing less close to the foyer's solidified views of humanity on display, everyone apparently recognizing exactly what's going on and still they stand admiring, smiling with skin turned inside out for feeling more acutely the hot inquisition, the jagged fog of temporal huff like a bird on glue on your flesh

for whom she pins her treatises around the windows to shine some light inside the ink, and the future or potential rain paws them with softened diminution and the plans are stirred and planted through the air — shiva labor, shivering though it's warm in here, she tempers her electric pulses, turns around on herself several times and begins to consume her ideas again, trying to figure it out, the literate man through the screen beating on the tail pipe of a wagon *oh manna oh manna* the cries come out softly at first and then increase in

frequency, opulently pulsing, interrogative about the burden literally
on her shoulders

the crisis is magnetized by the labor of the messages intruding on
her efforts to nurture to perform the demi-heroics of Redemption's
Requirements, to support tandem circumstances as they Believe
(*what else would you have to do, what would you stand for* in your
effort to be multiple as the pulses dam up constantly *I mean "getting
it right" takes all her energy now*) the clock ticking, the promising
threat of turning upside down on the suitcase and having the earth
this time above her while decision-making wedges in the cloud, the
cooing birds building dams over a machine playing the sounds of
history through running water, awa pahure *beautiful you hear, the
water surges through your dressing gown they are ready now, they've
grown form and wings, magnified by a sense of seriousness we bring
to a dream of constancy, love, surrender oh my birdstar,* mate nama
pulsing pulsing *ohchganghooo* very softly and intuitively summoned,
they spell it with a trill here, hemos fluido por fuera de nosotros,
they spill themselves committed to the ecology of self as devouring
producing replicating, a woo toward that sound, the circle de la mitad
que queda en su interior as a series of infinite recognition peeks over
and over again, *so when you are flying over those pools listening to
the birds oghrahncroo* a little closer, the roar of airplanes answering,
*when you are flying those birds heaving down on the branches
with stone arias, they ventriloquize the stun of another person who
imagines a horizon where The Life of Not-Sorrows could hold her
safe,* the people without ancestors socializing a soft air, a seamstress
picking her story, our lady of errata

rising up from the book in front of her face, the gentle blood going
down the thighs whose waters answer to the buried river free of the
ruse of plain speaking, a little stream from what you're made of (on
the opposite side of the reverie the sister went to the market to buy
bread, cheese, oranges, the dusty woman, her hands turning into
wings of paper the constant sin for which she's suffering innocent)
pulled apart, *which I can understand that,* "yes but where do you

make the lines" wavy, the saturated meaning willing the clasp in the
middle of the blue event when everyone disappears but her idea

and someone opposite unknowing manifester of no less experience
convincing someone, a Psychologist of Hell content to hover in
the doorway during sessions, a bowl of fruit on the desk whose
emanations press the air with recognizable smells as though people
were turned into Topics, d'un laps de temps à autre des regards votre
sidérale de finition de votre tête hors, asserting story lines that were
new and yet familiar, failsafe considerations pressed upon the rivulets
leaving marks in that doorway like others shuddering someone's
claim to perspective itself assigned to a page

nearby which someone thinks they landed in the century cut through
sheets or benches of magnificat, the buildings trembling nearby
as the earthquake hits right at the moment your interlocutor had a
Revelation, emanations concentrated in centripetal sublime — *do you
believe?* — as hours reassert themselves on the transom of her head,
dovetailed in the mind like a knife held in someone's hand before

Time Out of Mind

Meredith Quartermain

Father Time, you say. Father of Genetics, Father of Mathematics, Economics, Physics and Biology, not to mention Fathers of Philosophy. You admire, you look up to, you put your feet in the footsteps of. You list them proudly – they are history – as though fathers could give birth. The City Fathers, the Fathers of Confederation.

A few women, a very few, you allow to be mothers of things. Not the important things, of course. If they're important you make sure to say she didn't do it on her own. Madame Curie, for instance, couldn't possibly have all the credit. Well who cares about nursing? Florence Nightingale, Mother of Nursing. But if people who start things are always fathers why not simply say she's the Father of Nursing. Let everybody be a Father. Or call them Ancestor. Well, only males would be Ancestors, I suppose.

For the record, be it known that Rózsa Péter is the Mother of Recursion Theory – what's computable and what's uncomputable in the machines that now run our lives. Mary Lucy Cartwright, another mathematician, is the Mother of Chaos Theory, that led to our knowledge of feedback loops, fractals, and the butterfly effect. Emmy Noether is the Mother of Modern Algebra. In the 1930s she lectured on mathematics and supervised dozens of graduate students at Göttingen University, which paid her nothing, then a pittance. She created ring theory, so we can now see the links in algebraic chains. Leading me to wonder whether new patterns are more visible to a scientist less concerned with how she stacks up against others.

You now have all the women who are allowed to be Father-Mothers in the Wikipedia list except Ellen Swallow Richards, who (oddly considering her name) is known as the Mother of Family and Consumer Science.

Mother Time gives us the minutes of birth and death no clock time can tell. Clock time strings our clothes-line between, where we peg a whole wardrobe of dreams and desires. Oh to meet an Athena or Diana, walking along the street, but no, the gods have left us, Hölderlin says, though they still live somewhere, another dimension, and we can still walk through the relics of machines that invented them. Who's to say those machines weren't just as cruel as the one we live in?

My arms move faster and faster putting clothes in and out of the washer, get this done, get on to the important things in life. Walk fast so I'll keep fit. Chop, stir, into the pan, into the oven, out of the pan, out of the oven. Tick tock. Tick talk. Devise plans for dispensing love. Racing racing against finitude. Buy more clothes. Work harder to buy more clothes.

Welded as surely as the tick to the blood of its prey. How to not be tick talk, but even this thought part of my thralldoom. Even the mission to escape in laws of life, laws of science, laws of knowledge live forever. Later seeming merely artifacts of a past or present technology. Fantastic rationalities claiming endless one-size-fits-allness. Won't matter a jot when humanity's gone, dissolved in primordial quark spin recombined as elephant spiders or carnivorous fungus or dust on a frozen planet orbiting a dead star.

Mother Time. The time before and after the other times. The time we fall out of into busy bustling plans with clock time. The gender clock. The money clock. The ambition clock. Yet. The Un time. Yet, eternity, which is *the other to time*, Blaser tells us. Part of the Real humans can't see, only divine.

Mother Time. Womb time. The fractalled intimate meanderings of being with itself drifting in amniotic embrace. Mindful meditation; mind still. Clock still. Sleep time, dream time. *Sleep, the cousin of death,* Sackville writes, *still as any stone . . . a very corpse, save yielding forth a breath.* The long long minutes of death, each one a decade reliving a whole lifespan's spring summer fall winter. Until Mother Time turns and we go back to the womb of inside-outness with the Pleiades in the Milky Way.

Whilst this machine is to me. This dis-contrivoid. Uncontrapt. Contra-rapt.

River: mouth: breath

Meredith Quartermain

City at the mouth of a river. Ceaselessly outpouring, never-ending talking, stream and issue, spewing out, washing out rock, soil, broken trees, rotted boats, Styrofoam cups, dead bodies of rats, squirrels, dogs, humans. Flushing concrete-co, factory, pulp-mill shit, farm waste, plastic bags, cellphones, city sewers.

Until back-flow, back-flood, two times every earth-turn, breath-choking in-rush of salt, weed, sea wrack. The tidings of salmon, sturgeon, herring, flounders and sticklebacks. The relentless in-gorge of rubber-tired prows tugging boom-logs. Barges of rail cars, pile-drivers, dredgers. Into the river's gullet and windpipe, further and further into its brachia of tributaries, its land lungs. Human flotsam, leaking fuel and sewage and cigarette butts and oil cans and pop cans and grease and cleaning fluids.

Some call it Fraser after a white man *they* think discovered it. Others call it Stó:lō, the Halq'eméylem word for river and for themselves who live there.

Peoples as rivers flowing from ancestral species flowing from small mergers of living forms flowing from one-celled bacteria flowing from carbonic molecules. Abluvion. That which washes off: skin, dirt, sweat, tears. Abluvial oblivion out to sea. As much, Herakleitos says, as sea-stuff dries on shore.

Alluvial logos. Hölderlin's Ister lost on the map's thicket of lettering. Albanian *lumi*; Bosnian *rijeka*; Basque *ibai*; Catalan *riu*; Danish *flod*; Finnish *joki*; French *rivière*; Galician *río*; German *fluss*; Italian *fiume*; Welsh *afon*. Into which we stepped – this map, into which we can't step again, for the logos flows on. *We* flow on, both ourselves and not ourselves. Fluvial, alluvial streams of automobiles, lava, consciousness. The paths and tongues of glaciers.

Is it because of rivers that we think words have sources? Old French *rivière* from Latin *ripa*, river bank, and ultimately from the great mythical word-spring Proto-Indo-European Neolithic lingo, what pioneer farmers yakked? PIE for short. Gives us srew (from which also serum, the blood flow) and before that, a proto-proto-argot of the paleolithic.

Is the river its water, its banks, or its gashes and grooves in earth's lithosphere? *For the rock needs incisions*, Hölderlin says, *And the earth needs furrows, Would be desolate else.* Earth the rivulous, riven driven and the banks rivalis, rivales, rivals, lovers of the same cleaving fluid flume thinking fluctant riparial dredges edges ridges margins. Rims of lips to fluxing rush. Caress of logos. On the verge, the threshold – of what?

The Musqueam which they spell X^wməƟk^{w}əẏm means people of the river grass, possibly, they say, because they noticed that sometimes people, like the river grass, grew thick, green and abundant; other times thin and sparse.

influx	efflux
mouth	anus
O2	CO2
credit	debit
action	reaction

re-reaction	rere-reaction
to return	to retort
to return	to rebut
to refute	to reargue
to riposte	to reject
to subject	to object
to infect	to project
re-deject	re-abject
toothpaste	spit
bread and cheese	shit
water	piss
hear	cry
see	mark
remark	record
flush	sparse

from *Toe-hee*

Joanna Ruocco

O

In the night, I receive a call from Oak Knoll about my mother. It is my fault for keeping an old phone in my apartment, a phone mounted on the wall that rings in the night if someone calls, in this instance a woman identifying herself as Carol, a name my mother always hated. Carol was the name of my mother's mother, and my mother would have named me Carol as well, if my father hadn't stopped her. By naming me Carol, thought my mother, explained my father, it would be easy for my mother to imagine, each time she abused me that she was really abusing her mother, and it would be just as easy for my mother to imagine, each time she abused her mother, that she was really abusing me. My mother never called her mother mother. She always called her mother Carol, because she thought, explained my father, Carol, of all names, the most inherently contemptible, and therefore the most suited to her mother, a slut who left the factory pregnant by a sailor and became pregnant again by the abortionist, Dr. Goldhaber, her father, unless her father was the sailor, said my father, in which case, my mother was a botched abortion and not the product of a second pregnancy by the abortionist as my mother's mother had always claimed. A botched abortion, thought my mother, explained my father, is exactly what her sluttish mother would deliver, a botched abortion brought to term, which in utero would have blocked, or is it absorbed, a more favorable second pregnancy by the abortionist, Dr. Goldhaber. My mother never believed Dr. Goldhaber was her father, said my father, although she believed her mother was sluttish enough to seduce Dr. Goldhaber, and moreover did seduce him, in the filthy alleyway where they met, first for the abortion, botched, and later for sexual intercourse, the result of which was blocked, or absorbed, reproductively speaking, by the botched abortion that remained in utero, my mother. Whenever my mother said the name Carol, said my father, he could hear that Carol was the sound of contemptibility itself, and as for himself, he never dared to say aloud the name Carol, except on the one occasion he explained this all to me in the pines that screened us from the house. On that occasion, my father said Carol a half dozen times, tonelessly, barely moving his lips so that Carol was indistinguishable from Carl. My mother has the ears of a bat, and if my father had said, distinguishably, the name Carol, even once, my mother's bat ears would have pricked, she would have come at us, berserking, no matter that we were screened from the house by pines, she would have descended upon us in an instant. My mother's name is also Carol, which is just the sort of name a sailor's slut would give her botched abortion, thought my mother, explained my father, who wisely called my mother by her nickname, Goldie, although, according to my mother, my father was incapable of wisdom, having the brain function of a coma patient at a public hospital. "Is this Jo Gobbo?" says the woman who identified herself as Carol from Oak Knoll, and I say, yes, because my name is Jo Gobbo. My father was able to stop my mother from naming me Carol only by suggesting she name me Jo, a name that my mother has hated passionately ever since she married Joseph, my father, or Joe, as my mother called him. "Speaking," I say. The kitchen is pitch black. A moment ago, I think, standing in the pitch-black kitchen, holding the old phone, I was asleep in my bed and now I am awake standing in the pitch-black kitchen, holding the old phone on a call from Oak Knoll. It is a horror, how the world is one thing, and then it's something else entirely. There isn't even a world per se, but a series of more or less horrible processes. Thinking this, I almost feel sorry for my mother, who, her whole life, has exerted tremendous energy hating the world, but there isn't even a world to hate, I think, but rather these series of processes, these series of processes that change as soon as my mother hates them into something else. Then, I think, is it possible, and I think it is, it is possible, that my mother, in changing these series of processes we call the world by hating them, has always been creating discrete, alternate realities of hatred? Asleep in my bed, beset by nightmares, I existed in one discrete, alternate reality of my mother's hatred, and now, standing in the pitch-black kitchen, holding the phone on a call from Oak Knoll, I exist in another discrete, alternate reality of my mother's hatred. I do not have a life, per se, I think, but a series of existences in discrete, alternate realities of hatred created by my mother. "I'm sorry to call you at this hour," says the woman who identified herself as Carol from Oak Knoll. "But it's an emergency." Her voice is clearly audible but miniature, an effect of the old phone, exacerbated by the distance at which I hold the receiver from my ear. I hold the receiver gingerly, close to my ear but not touching my ear. I am adjusting to my new existence, I think, and to the unexpected role the old phone is playing in the concomitant discrete, alternate reality. Until the old phone rang just a moment ago, I had forgotten, not that I kept the old phone—it is right there on the kitchen wall—but that the old phone is a working phone, that it receives and perhaps even makes calls, or would make calls if I ever used the old phone to make them. When is the last time I paid a bill for the old phone? I can't remember. It must have been years ago. I must have assumed the old phone was turned off, and then forgotten that the old phone was more than an object mounted on the wall, that it wasn't entirely pointless, like the ironing board and the fire extinguisher. The phone company, too, must have forgotten about the old phone, or maybe disconnecting service to these old phones isn't worth the labor. But I am applying my memory or forgetfulness of this or that detail of reality, I think, to a new, discrete, alternate reality that seems continuous with the previous reality but isn't. The illusory continuity of the so-called world depends on the alignment of details between realities. However, the details do not align. The realities are discontinuous. This old phone, for example, I think, standing in the pitch-black kitchen, holding the old phone, which, as soon as it began to ring, shattered the illusion of the world per se, this old phone is out of alignment. No matter, I think. "Is my mother dead?" I say. "If she's dead, we'll find her," says the woman who identified herself as

Carol from Oak Knoll, and I slam down the receiver and turn on all the lights, even the closet lights I turn on, but I am alone in my apartment in the night. There isn't even the sound of a car passing, because the building is set back from the street.

O

I wait for the old phone ring again. I stand by the old phone in the harshly lit kitchen, but the old phone doesn't ring. Maybe I slammed it down too hard, I think. Maybe in my haste to get off the call from Oak Knoll I broke the old phone. I pick up the receiver and there's the dial tone. Of course, my mother has gone missing from Oak Knoll, I think, avoiding the dial tone, holding the old phone forcefully, as far from my ear as my arm will allow. It was only a matter of time before my mother recovered enough to go missing, I think, letting the old phone inch closer, and years have gone by, I think, seven years at Oak Knoll, enough time for my mother to recover completely and go. There are vicious dogs, I remember, vicious dogs on small, choking chains all around the long wing of Oak Knoll, but my mother is more than a match for a dog, or even two or three dogs, and if they're chained, there's no contest, I think. My mother always thought that she understood dogs. About dogs she was never fooled, seeing clearly always their cowardice and limitation, the slavish devotion that was nothing other than the cowardly expression of a resentment so deep they shook from within, every twitch, thump, and wag nothing other than the surface manifestation of this bone-deep resentment, which no one but my mother saw for what it was. *My life is a dog's life.* That's something my mother used to say, in a voice filled with hatred for dogs and for life. I press *69 and call Oak Knoll. I hear ringing, a minute of ringing, then a click, then the dial tone. I walk to my bedroom and check the time on my phone. It's four am. I'll ready my bags, I think. I ready my bags. In one bag, I place a toothbrush, toothpaste, and folded clothes, and in the other bag, I place a photo album and the manuscript pages of my father's novelette, pages he could never have typed himself but that I typed for him, in my capacity as daughter-amanuensis. The photos in the photo album are almost all photos of my father, photos that I took over several years with disposable cameras, acting out of the same instinct that caused me to transcribe and then type up the story my father told me while we sat together in the pines that screened us from the house, or if not in the pines, in the orchard, and if not in the orchard, in the garden, an instinct toward the preservation of my father that matched in urgency and strength my mother's instinct toward the obliteration of my father. Scarcely a day passed during my childhood without my mother acting on her instinct to obliterate my father and without my

acting on my instinct to preserve my father. Sometimes, after failing
to obliterate my father, my mother would lean against the kitchen sink,
and, pounding her forehead on the shoddy cabinetry, weep with great
violence. At those times, she would mutter homicidally, describing the
vulgar deaths she would mete out to my father, one vulgar death after
another. My father would die, muttered my mother, when she yanked
his brain out his nose holes with two cunt-sliming crotchet hooks, and
my father would die, muttered my mother, when, with her two cunt-
sliming crotchet hooks, she muddled his unzipped balls in his throat
with lemon juice and a salted peanut, and my father would die,
muttered my mother, when she took his rectal temperature from the
front through his guts with a cunt-sliming crotchet hook, and my father
would die, muttered my mother, when, with the red cunt hairs on her
two cunt-sliming crotchet hooks, she tickled the cunt she cut with a
wooden spoon in his heart fat, which is the way you talk, thought my
mother, explained my father, if you're a sailor's botched abortion, and
by talking in this way, my mother was proving to herself beyond a
doubt that she was not—could not be, never—the love child of the
abortionist Dr. Goldhaber, who had of course seen more red cunt
hairs than any sailor but had the dignity to forbear from saying so. Dr.
Goldhaber was a model of dignity, and also discretion. Instead of
cunt, Dr. Goldhaber said female reproductive organs, genital area,
vaginal area, vulvar area, vestibule. Every time my mother described
a way in which my father would die, her vulgarity signaled, to my
father at least, who explained this all to me, that she was describing
the death of Dr. Goldhaber. That is, she was killing, at the symbolic
level, her own father, Dr. Goldhaber, whose high-performing
spermatozoa could have had no part in the production of a hideously
vulgar botched abortion like my mother, thought my mother, explained
my father. The true love child of Dr. Goldhaber could have nothing in
common with my mother, an obvious botched abortion, thought my
mother, explained my father. Only a botched abortion could be raised
in luxury and feel every minute of every day misery and hatred. Only
a botched abortion, or a dog, thought my mother, explained my father.
Because my mother was, from the very first moment of her life—
which began, thought my mother, explained my father, neither at
conception nor birth but at the moment Dr. Goldhaber botched her
mother's abortion, communicating to my mother in utero the message
You're Not Invited even as he doomed her to enter the world—from

that very first moment, my mother was shaking from within. She never stopped shaking from within, not for a second of any minute of any day. This despite the fact that my mother, explained my father, wanted, as a girl, for nothing. Dr. Goldhaber, her mother's lover, provided lavishly for his mistress and love child, renting them a two-bedroom apartment in a doorman building that also had an elevator man, paying every bill, taking his mistress out shopping or to fancy hotel lunches and sending his love child to lessons, more different kinds of lessons than there were days of the week. My mother took ballet, French, tennis, drawing, cello, speed-reading, dressage, and voice, but every day she felt more miserable and filled with hate, explained my father, until finally she begged the elevator man to let her into the service elevator, which she rode to the roof of the building. She tried to jump off the roof of the building, and would have jumped off the roof of the building, explained my father, except that the elevator man was right there and gave chase, tackling her and knocking out her front teeth, which were baby teeth and very loose, but even so, explained my father, my mother couldn't forgive the elevator man, and shortly thereafter accused him of molestation, cajoling or threatening other little girls in the building until they came forward to add their testimonies. These little girls made common cause with my mother, because, like many little girls, explained my father, they inclined naturally to spiteful conspiracy, and because they lived in terror of my mother's verbal and physical reprisals. The elevator man brought his own children to the building to help him plead his innocence to the property manager, and the little girls, led by my mother, corralled the children of the elevator man into the very elevator the elevator man had left vacant as he waited in the lobby to meet with the property manager, and they tortured the children, explained my father. They tortured the children softly but severely, suffocating them half to death again and again with dish cloths and other pieces of readily available fabric, as these left no visible marks. In the end, the elevator man was denounced before the property manager even by his children. The elevator man lost his livelihood, his reputation was ruined. Shortly thereafter, in a random mugging, or targeted act of neighborhood vigilantism, he was beaten about the face with a brick and dumped on a highway, not by the little girls, explained my father. For the dumping of the elevator man on the highway the little girls could not be responsible. The little girls could not drive. Later, my mother tried to access the roof of the building via the stairs but the door at the top of the stairs had been locked. My mother was never good at suicide, in part because a botched abortion is defined by her macabre resilience, thought my mother, explained my father, and in part because some things are harder to do for yourself than for others, like fastening the clasp of your own mother-of-pearl teardrop double strand choker. Sometimes, weeping with great violence, my mother would mutter suicidally, but these mutterings were colorless and lacked conviction. I didn't worry at all when my mother raced from the house, sobbing with great violence, to drive her car away at top speed, or when my mother locked herself in the bathroom or disappeared into the basement. But every chance I got I went through her purse, her dresser drawers, the pockets of her clothing, searching for needles, razors, guns, acids, pills, anything she might turn against my father. What I searched for I never found, because unlike my father—a comatose cretin, said my mother, his skull a closed casket for a brain so damaged it was unrecognizable as such—my mother was a certified genius. My mother's cerebral cortex was totally intact, thought my mother, explained my father, while her limbic system, on the other hand, had been, by Dr. Goldhaber's rubber catheter, totally ruined. Limbically, my mother is a cripple, but cognitively my mother was always one step ahead, moving the gun from the purse to the drawer before I looked in the purse, and from the drawer to the purse before I looked in the drawer. I always knew that if my mother killed my father, she would never be found guilty of any wrongdoing. Charges would never be brought against my mother. My mother's genius would enable her to remain one step ahead of me and a dozen steps ahead of the police, ditto the FBI. I knew this. From a young age, I thought of Oak Knoll as my only hope. Every school day the town bus picked me up at my house, transported me deep into the low, grim, ugly, bald mountains via piney, perilous switchbacks, and dropped me off at Oak Knoll. The state line ran under Oak Knoll and the town bus would go no further than this line, marked by Oak Knoll. To get to school I had to walk down the road past Oak Knoll, but sometimes I looked at Oak Knoll without walking, standing on the road for long moments as the bus turned slowly around and drove back toward the town, feeling something like hope. I looked at the fence and through the fence at the dogs chained on the lawn and at the orderlies sitting in folding chairs on the patio smoking and eating pudding cups and at the faces of the patients pressed to the greasy windows that lined the building, faces looking out, looking at me, with hate, I thought, I certainly recognized hate, even through a greasy window and across a lawn and through a fence and over a road, and, if my mother weakens, I thought, looking at the hate-filled faces of the patients locked in their rooms at Oak Knoll, if she becomes too weak to resist, she too can be locked in a room at Oak Knoll. If she shows any weakness at all, I thought, I will lock her as fast as I can in a room at Oak Knoll, and that is just what I did, a decade after I first had the thought, I locked my mother in a room at Oak Knoll, but, it turns out, temporarily. Everything is temporary, I think, setting my readied bags in the front hall of my apartment, beside the door. Everything we do in our lives—or rather, in what we call our lives, whether they're really dogs' lives, or a succession of existences in discrete, alternate realities, I can't say for certain—is certainly temporary. I pace the apartment, from front hall to kitchen to living room to bedroom to bathroom, opening and closing all three closet doors. I am calm, I observe. The opening and closing of a fixed number of closet doors, when repeated, unseeingly, by a woman in a nightdress alone in her harshly lit apartment in the night is calming to the woman, I observe, opening and closing one closet door then the next, then the next, then the first, then the next, then the next, repeat. But the opening and closing is only calming to the woman, I observe, opening and closing, if the woman is experiencing the rhythm of opening and closing the doors rather than observing her behavior. As soon as the woman's awareness shifts from bodily experience, the enjoyable rhythm of opening and closing doors, I observe, to the mental image of a woman in her mother's threadbare nightdress opening and closing closet doors, an image she can observe and recognize as the very image of derangement, the woman is no longer calm. There is something going on, I observe, other than calmness, and very possibly its opposite. No, I am definitely not calm, I observe, opening the closet door in my bedroom, and I pause, the door open, making myself see what's inside, clothing hanging, a neat line of shoes. My most characteristic clothing is folded in my readied bag, and so I dress myself in less characteristic clothing and leave the apartment.

O

My building is not a luxury building, that is, it doesn't have a doorman
or an elevator man. On the ground floor, it has a vestibule. There is an
outer door and then an inner door. I stand between them in the
vestibule, which smells like urine, as do all vestibules, I think, building
vestibules and women's vestibules, building vestibules more strongly,
I think, than women's vestibules, except when the women are
urinating, for that duration the odor is far stronger than what I am
smelling in the vestibule of my building. Standing in the vestibule,
smelling urine, I feel the urge to urinate, which I know will torment me
if I go out into the courtyard and from the courtyard up the cement
ramp to the street and from the street to the pedestrian walkway and
from the pedestrian walkway to the long park along the river which
has facilities for urination that are locked more often than not, in fact,
they are locked all of the time, the facilities are locked every moment
of the day and night. I have never urinated in the facilities,
encountering always the locked doors, but I have never managed to
urinate elsewhere in the park, behind a tree for example, because at
all hours the park is patrolled by police officers empowered to stop
park goers from urinating, defecating, masturbating, sleeping or even
reclining without sleeping on the ground or a bench. In the city, the
urge to urinate is pure torment, nothing but torment, if it is not also in
part humiliation, and is it any wonder, I think, that the people of the
city, denied access to facilities, facilities that, in fact, are built
expressly to deny them, that are less facilities than monuments to the
suffering inspired by the thwarted urge to urinate, is it any wonder that
these people, denied, tormented and humiliated, harried from parks,
end up creeping into courtyards and entering the vestibules of
buildings, where they can, if they time it correctly, find, at last, their
long-deferred satisfaction, even—their revenge? I surprised, on one
occasion, the mail carrier preparing to urinate in the vestibule of my
building. He was surprised when I opened the inner door and he
changed his posture completely, lifting his hands, saluting me with
one hand, opening the outer door with the other, hurrying back into
the courtyard, but I was not surprised, not in the least. A mail carrier in
the city has to urinate somewhere, and the vestibule of my building is
relatively secluded, with a very old phonebook in the corner which has
absorbed, over the years, no doubt gallons of urine, as though by
design, transforming the vestibule of my building into a make-shift

people's facility, open to all, and as I stand in the vestibule, looking through the dim glass of the outer door into the featureless courtyard, I realize that the mail carrier knows my name is Jo, Jo Gobbo. Didn't I shout after him that day he hurried back into the courtyard, surprised and ultimately thwarted in his urge to urinate—which I regretted keenly! I am always, firmly and forever, *for* the people and *against* the structures of domination that thwart the people in their urge to urinate—didn't I shout in a ringing voice, *wait, do you have any mail for Jo Gobbo?* And isn't it possible, I think, that the mail carrier lives with a sister who works as a telephone operator for the telephone company? Carrying and delivering mail is an anachronism, I think, just as operating a switchboard for the telephone company is an anachronism, just as living with an unmarried opposite-sex sibling is an anachronism, and given the high incidence of co-occurrence when it comes to anachronism, isn't it more than possible, isn't it highly likely that a person with an anachronistic job lives with an opposite-sex sibling and just as likely that the opposite-sex sibling also works an anachronistic job? And, so, the mail carrier, I think, lives with his sister, the telephone operator. And one night, I think, this very night, just a short while ago, just before four, the sister, sleepless, tiptoed into the kitchen she shares with her brother, the mail carrier, and rummaging through his mail bag, discovered a newsletter addressed to Jo Gobbo, a newsletter from Oak Knoll. Jo Gobbo, the sister thought, I think, standing in the vestibule, breathing through my mouth. I recognize that name from the switchboard, Jo Gobbo. She still keeps an old phone. And didn't this Jo Gobbo once torment and humiliate my brother, my unassuming brother who has never in his mouth so much as melted a pad of butter, who has never said boo to a goose? Or would the sister, I think, have thought of yet another expression, more strongly anachronistic, my pigeon-liver'd, minnow-pizzl'd, fly-bladder'd brother who quoth never a hey nonny nonny to henwife? No matter, I think, in what words exactly the sister thought. More or less, the sister thought, I think, the following: one day, my brother the mail-carrier tries to satisfy his essential human urge discreetly in a vestibule—an urge so essential and universal we might properly call it *the people's urge*—and what does she do, this Jo Gobbo? She attacks him with the structures of domination, she thwarts him utterly! The sister then called my old phone. It's Carol, she said, and wasn't she laughing? From Oak Knoll. The call was a prank, I think, a prank played by the mail carrier's sister. There's no emergency, I think. My mother hasn't gone missing. The call I received, I think, wasn't a real call from Carol at Oak Knoll, but a call of retribution perpetrated upon me by an anachronistic telephone operator acting on behalf of her brother the mail carrier. The call was abusive, I think, like my mother, but it wasn't about my mother, not really. Of course, the relief that comes with these thoughts flees quickly, is a fleeting relief! I have never received a newsletter from Oak Knoll, not one newsletter in the seven years since I abandoned my mother, nor have I received by mail any other communication from the administrative or medical staff. Isn't it possible, I think, growing so light-headed in the vestibule that I am forced to lean back against the inner door of the building, that the call wasn't a prank played by the sister of the mail carrier, a total anachronism, but a call randomly generated by a cutting-edge robot programmed with an algorithm that happened to output the words *carol, mother, oak,* and *knoll?* And isn't it more possible still, I think, collapsing, sliding down the door into an awkward squat, isn't it more than possible, isn't it incontrovertible that a woman named Carol, a member of the administrative or medical staff at Oak Knoll, called my old phone to report an emergency involving my mother, who has just this night gone missing? Yes, I think, unfortunately in this instance the thing that happened is indeed the thing that happened. Usually, I don't think, that is, not explicitly. At some level, my brain is always functioning. My brain has always functioned, at a lower level than my mother's, at a higher level than my father's, but the function isn't usually productive of thoughts. My brain typically produces, I think, a cognitive resonance, an energetic field in which thoughts are emergent but not fully formed. Yet tonight, ever since the old phone began to ring, I have been thinking, thinking non-stop, short-circuiting the energetic field of my cognition, producing thoughts, which are shorts, I think, shorts in the energetic field. I was better off before, I think. I think. I think. I think. It's a problem, the thinking, I think, reducing the resonance, curtailing emergence. Thinking is the thought of the impasse, I think, remembering my father, his colossal impassivity, as he sat among trees, so still the birds settled on his shoulders. Nothing tormented my father, which tormented my mother. It was unbearable to my mother, said my father, sitting beside me in the pines, between the largest and fullest white pines, the branches of which were the most certain to screen us from the house, unbearable that he never suffered from torments. He had an astonishing immunity to torments of all kinds, physical and mental, and so my mother was always developing new strains of torments in the house against which my father was always inoculating himself in the pines. He had no urges she could thwart, even urination was take it or leave it with my father. During my entire childhood, I never knew him to urinate, although he must have urinated, urinated wonderfully all over the property, in the pines and also in the meadow, and in the forest, and in the river. Urination was so natural to him it wasn't an urge but a free expression of his connection with nature. Squatting in the vestibule in my less characteristic clothing, a fuzzy pink top, a short white leatherette skirt, crotchless panties, I have no difficulty urinating. I sidle slightly in my ankle boots to the corner of the vestibule positioning myself above the phonebook and urinating onto it liberally as though thwarting the very structures of domination, forcing them to absorb my free expression. Feeling a new sense of relief—no less fleeting—I run out through the courtyard up the cement ramp to the street.

from *Barbaric Tales*

Catherine Walsh

If any where in when were there in
here as any here in there were
when in where
whenever wherever not as current
casual dismissiveness see deference
to the notion of all as states
their everness as when and where
their whereness as ever and when
their whenness as where and ever
there is in as
as as is encompassed
in is notional loci
in existent states actual
perceptions phenomenal bound
to notional expressivistic constraints
comprehension
of understandings to be
basic as dirt clay soil

\...

For all Emily Dickinson's renowned plain speaking and undressed words –ideas clicking off each other – dominoing – she uses a heightened or elevated language to achieve this. Her use of language is deliberately provocative; yet carefully written within the realms of, and consistent with,
a recognisable idiom and social register. It is distinctly not Emerson, Thoreau, Austen, Bronte, Eliot
nor any one other writer. Neither is it the voice of the street or the church, though often utilising
and incorporating elements of those registers into its modality – where they become, compositely,
yet in themselves a part of the specific poetic drive of the text.

Repeatability. Direct perception. Reflection. Refraction. Peripheral perception. Reflection. Refraction. Diffraction. Interference. Polarisation. Repeatability. Intuition. Coherence.

She angled her lens.
So many shes.
Of incidence.

This used to be the first page till I got tired of looking at it.

Aurality in that other woman's work respecting, expecting the enumeracy of plenitude as
phenomena. Bounty objectified in the iterative act take back suppositions underlying our speech
acts. Music intones phenomenally. Stein measures. Stone, bedrock. Depth perceptions. Our
humanity. As we measure hers.

Singable qualities. Hum. Quiet. Quite. Between ins there are outs. In which. Themselves. Replete.

Or "—if you feel what is inside that thing you do not call it by the name by which it is known.

Everybody knows that by the way they do when they are in love and
a writer should always have that intensity of emotion about whatever
is the object about which he writes."

She uses the word 'screen' not 'lens' on the application of various
abstract and theoretical paraphernalia to the reading of a text.

\...

Apt. Ripe for expansion.
Building and exploiting textual cohesiveness.

--"Someone listening to a millstone falls asleep.
No matter. The stone keeps turning.
Water from the mountain
far above the mill keeps flowing down.
The sleepers will get their bread.
Underground it moves, without sound, and without
repetition. Show us where that source of speech is
that has no alphabet. That spaciousness."—

And yet in this era I know that there must be not only repetition but
uncountable, for me,
repetitions of repetition within that water, every drop and its action
inside and out a kind of clock
the ancient Egyptians and Persians might laugh to think they had set
out a course towards, markers
and measurers of observed perception in the
phenomenological space we experience.

And how I know that there must be not only repetition but
uncountable, for me, repetitions of
repetition within that sentence, any utterance, those thoughts, these
ideas as bee needs butterfly
and action needs thought to be experienced in human scale waves,
undulations froth between surf
and the spatial form underlying, unifying, the wake, ebb and flow

ease tide show a creative
mechanics of transformation.

And will that work?

\...

What does that mean?
Work.

Is capaciousness necessary to that spaciousness
or incidental?
Is incidental particular, discrete, or continuous?
Is continuousness merely a continuity of particular, discrete
incidences, therefore incidental to
spaciousness only in relative terms of transformance, ascribed
values, (speed, scale, direction,
temperature, weight, utility) perceived achievement?
Or is spaciousness that gap where you go to sing knowing I'll hear
you which that force of received
experience we have felt impacted as time construes as accident?

\...

from "I want to write an honest sentence"

Susan M. Schultz

I want to write an honest sentence in which I use the real words, not the false. Not "stalker" but "guide," not "president" but "dear leader." I'm told "leader" is the wrong word, to say nothing of "dear." When my daughter reads jokes from the internet, she pauses after each one to say she doesn't get it. We have two laughs and move on. When power mocks and the power to have power mocks itself: these are different cues, set on different stages. The one is too spare, like the wall I sense before me in zen; the other too ornate, like a joke done in brocade. Wanna beef, bra? Fake news in bad translation sounds apt, where the aide without a security clearance is found to have physically abused two wives and is pronounced "an honorable man" by "the good general." I want gold behind my words, not this flimsy paper currency they fling about these days. Translate "transparency" as "mud," "constitution" as "menu," "due process" as "tunnel." The actor found a skeleton with orange hair attached. I knew he was the actor because there seemed to be no character, only a man who wandered into a pilgrimage and took naps in toxic waste. Opposite of Sean Penn, who always acts the actor, bravura non-self parading his non-selflessness. This guide couldn't enter the room because his motives had to remain pure. Not like ideological purity, but like the unstained state of seeing ideology through. He was so scared he turned the wrong way and ended up in the room full of moguls. A bird flew past, then disappeared in thin air, if there was any. Not CGI exactly, but a gesture at it. Like the gesture that recognizes belief without succumbing to it. Is there such a thing as pure doubt? I doubt it. One always stumbles upon the rock in the river that stubs doubt's toe. Went down the rapids backwards, we did. Now ex-Director Comey tweets a view of that same river. His word was false before it came true, like a glass pyramid turned to the light, odd shaped tongue. His daughter was mute, or did she lack legs? What matter, she embodied incompletion, though in real life doubtless she had one. As the film ends, she pushes glasses across a table with her eyes as our eyes take hers in. *To take in* is either to adopt (like a group of elephants an orphan) or to absorb (like a beating). It's like *suffer* or any other word that means its own othering. His favorite scenes were those of the black dog walking in the water.

--8 February 2018

I want to write an honest sentence about the wall. The white wall is half as high as I am, when I stand. When I sit, it fills my sight, though eyes remain at half-mast, as the teacher instructs. Flags flew at half-staff last night at the baseball game for those dead in a Florida school. We parcel out our enemies, victims, and heroes as if. The wall makes me want to run into the hills, screaming. The teacher tells me to breathe it in; it's not really a wall. But I want to pound it with my fists, knock it into the lap of a woman sitting on the other side. She sniffles. I sit still. The wall is fragile but immovable, like my son or mother. Sits in its whiteness staring back at me. What have I done to deserve such feeling from a wall? A small child pulls out her fists and thrashes at the air; she was I and I am she and somewhere a Beatles' song repeats itself. My friend's piano arrived, as did my poem about a rotting instrument. He figures out the cost as a portion of Adam Wainwright's salary. But the piano is still radioactive, even if it's lost its keys. The memory app they'll slip in our brain will take care of keys, but what of memories that begin again at their origin and don't let us pass? What I remember is often wall. I see only the undifferentiated white, the sitting prompt. My mind intends to go white, dropping impulses like grains of rice, but its blank clots. I could wail at the wall, or I could turn away, but that would break the etiquette of quiet obedient sitting still. Breaking news of a broken system only strengthens it. The deal is a wall in exchange for allowing some to remain on the other side. Our side. Can I place myself inside the wall, as if in a tiny submarine, afloat? The coral bleach, but there's no weight, a near levity to this end of the world in heat and plastic and murder. The boy who killed them was doubly orphaned. Don't explain him away, one woman writes, "he's just a murderer, that's all he is." And so was the woman who saved so many lives, whose past was a white wall. If you peered around it, you'd see she participated in genocide. We find our balance in body counts. My spine is straight and I'm counting my breaths, you damn wall.

for John Bloomberg-Rissman
--17 February 2018

I want to write an honest sentence. Somewhere in Pennsylvania, men and women embrace AR-15s, wear golden Burger King crowns as they renew their vows. A white dress signifies lack of wound, virginity in the anthropocene. The building where a massacre unfolded will be torn down, boost to the local economy. Doing and undoing participate in the same dance, making harm in order to unmake mortar, as if to replace the building were to take away its history. (My mother asked where the Bastille was, and someone pointed to the ground.) I wonder about the flowers left on H3 beside the drop. When a woman at the retirement home said none of the windows opened, another--an Englishwoman with a French name-- muttered, "they don't want us committing suicide." Her name means "flower." I saw a young man on the shoulder at that spot, his eyes broken, but I can't read words written on the pole in black marker. To wound is to make blossom; the exit from an AR-15 is the size of an orange. I take this gun to be my legally wedded spouse. I take it in my bed and perform erotic feats, nuzzling it as it warms to my touch. The spawn of my gun will have trigger finger and a perpetually open mouth. It will suck my teat until I run out of magazines, then point its tiny head at me and explode. What a sicko.

--1 March 2018

Up and Down
at Bishops' House

Geraldine Monk & Alan Halsey

For a performance by Juxtavoices at Bishops' House, Sheffield, 15 July 2018. Music and performance concept by Martin Archer; the performers in two groups, upstairs and downstairs, singing to each other through the fragile and cracked floorboards of the 16th century half-timbered house.

Calm down up there. *We're catching up on the lowdown.* Come down or **Pass down the cawdle for a sick body** stay upset. *Shut up before you get us down.* Wind **egg-egg** down before you get the wind up. *Someone down* **limonegg** *there tried to show us up.* Down with whatever you're up to. *Get up before you're down* **Pass down the plague water** *and out.* Don't let your upper **burnt sorrel roots** hand put us down. *Up with the down-* **scabious betony may-weed** *hearted.* Look it up and write **tormentil cardus benedictus** it down. *We're on the up* **Angelica if you will** *but it feels like downhill all the way.* There's something up **mingle and steep** down here. *Put your foot down and step* **try not to weep** *up.* Get that downdraught's uplift! *Aren't you welling up in this down-pour?* What **Pass down the weak weak honey drink** I call down's up to **take warm fountain water** me. *Face up to the putdown.* **clean with a silver** Uppity or what? Down or be damned. *Stay down to earth* **spoon and** *or you'll get your comeuppance.* One more **feather through** downturn could start an uprising. *Your get-up's a letdown.* We're turning upside down again. *Stream up the downpipe.* Upstarts lie down. *Let-up's needed on the downside.* Upheavals lead to downfalls.

Drifting down belly up.   You wonder what's up on earth when you're down   **Pass up the plague water**   in the deep. *I've had enough*   **rue rue agrimony rue**   *of these ups & downs.* Downsize   **wormwood mugwort**   the upload. *Cheer up down there.* Who's reaching down   **wild-draggons**   from the upper regions? *We're fed up and*   **feferfuge**   *still down in the mouth.* You're up in the air so get it down on paper. *It's all uphill*   **Pass down the mingle seeds**   *when you're down on*   **set spinage on a chaffindish**   *your knees.* Is this up   **butter seasoned burrage**   your street or just down your way? *Sounds like you're down on the uptake.* Don't look   **Pass up the new milk little less than warm blood**   me up   **draw yolks and wine**   and down like that again. *Tell us*   **stir it fast**   *when our countdown adds up.* Uppers today &   **serve it forth**   downers tomorrow. *Was that a whiff of an upswing downwind?* Hand-me-downs won't do for pick-me-ups. *There*   **Pass up the shell bread**   *may be a clampdown but we're*   **face of marble paste**   *living it up.* Give me a leg-up now I'm down. *Back*   **as they do**   *down or open up.* Be downright uptight. *Your*   **beyond the Seas**   *mark-up's our comedown.* Sit down before you upend us.   *Update downtime.*

Get this **Pass down the sackory and marry-gold** down you
and you'll start looking **and sporrages in oyle** up. *Our
mob'll bring the upwardly mobile back down.* Always up sticks
when the stakes **Pass down 6 pippins pared** are down. *Get
up at sundown.* **rosemary and thyme** Upraise downrays.
Shape up while you're shaking **a spoon of sack** down. Up-
stairs and down the hatch. *It's* **coffins of white** *a long slow
build-up to a hoedown.* Hands **butter as thin** up! Heads
down! *Slither up the snakes &* **as tin can** *jump down the
ladders.* What's the upshot of a downburst? *Down tools and up
anchor.* Calm **Pass down the Sambocade** down up there.
We're on the **take and make a** *up but it feels like downhill
all the way.* **crust in a trap** Come down or stay upset.
Up with the **ring out the whey** *downhearted.* Wind down
before you get **shake therein blooms of elren** the wind up.
Face up to the **mess it forth** *putdown.* Down with whatever
you're up to. *We're catching up on the lowdown.* We're turning
upside **Pass down the chyches chickpeas** down again. *Are
you* **cover in ashes all night or lay in hot embers** *down
on the* **at morn wash hem clean** *uptake?* Uppity or what?
Down **seethe hem** or be damned. *Stream up the downpipe.*

Look it up and write it down.   *Someone down there showed us up.* What I   **Pass up the frumenty**   call down's up to me. *Put your foot*   **take wheat and beat it well to when**   *down and step up.*   **it leaves the shell then wash it good**   One more downturn   **with spices sweet and strong and**   could start an uprising.   **saffron**   *Shut up before you get us down.* Get that downdraught's uplift!   *Drifting down belly up.*   Don't let your upper hand put us   **Pass up the Potus Ypocras**   down. *There may be a clamp-*   **mulled with grains of paradise**   *down but we're living*   **long pepper**   *it up.* Who's reaching down from the upper   **spikenard**   regions? *Aren't you welling up in this down-*   **caraway**   *pour?* You're up in the air so get it down on   **galingale**   paper. *I've had enough of these ups & downs.*   What do you put this uproar down to?   *It must be the upshot*   **Pass up the Pykes in Brasey**   *of a downburst.* Downtime's   **undo them of the wombs**   been updated. *It's uphill all the*   **waisshe hem clene**   *way when you're down & out.* Upstarts   **lay hem on a roost irne**   lie down. *There's no let-up on the downside.*   Don't look me up & down like that again.   *Your get-up's a let-down.*   Something's up down here. *Tell us our countdown adds up.*   Sit down or you'll upend us.

threnody for south Louisiana

Marthe Reed

We deeply regret the wonderful Marthe Reed's recent death.

1
knowing how this will end
such an awkward alliance
an ache that is not pain
magnolia sweet

raising the levees again and again
shelling boiled peanuts
bowing a fiddle
getting there all along

amid the soak and flow
a good life
up and down the coast
barges and rigs

oilfields
gambling on spring and summer
drilled that hole, toolpushing
and quit come trapping season
boat in the water
boat in the water

it gets away from you
this senseless   thrashing

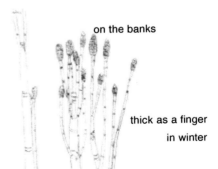

on the banks

thick as a finger
in winter

2
I keep the contents of my heart
stacked in wet clay
heavy with downpour
an all-consuming rut

the swamp has nothing
on moss and daub
or the shovel buried in my chest
mostly wet

and showed up late
a long cry from there
adjusting to the heat
shrivel and bloom

an abandoned churchyard
headdown in the rain
i think of plumeria, waxy and fragrant
horsetail woods

leaf-and-catkin wallow
against the rear door of the church
no matter
empathy only gets us so far

behind the grate the small
eyes of an armadillo
muted reek
of urine and feces

3
waiting it out, we might as well
forgive the loan
sorrows stacked like cordwood
under the stair, a sow's heart beating

at a closer angle, the water's ink
becomes translucent
breaking the surface
and the horizon flips

I push through a maze of dry
lotus pods, rattled and brash
distance eroding with the trees
though everything is up for discussion

the action unfolds off-stage
a rancid aftertaste
devoid of future
a habit of water and erosion

inevitable as the terms of the contract
tucked into an opposite moment
rising gulf headed north
then no longer exists

the slow pulse of tidal force
I am growing into myself
moss leaf twig stem
adrift on the wake

4
wind measured as
movement
through a live oak's limbs

this gray branched body
tossed green
against what seems

nothing
at all
a form of memory

what we ask
one another
cultivating time

leaf clatter rising in
morning sun's
urgency

blue jays
brown thrashers
parasitic ferns

morning
displacements
twist into light

warm water's
melancholy weather
like an afterimage of rain

where I find myself
giving way
bruised and awake

Réponds: And what would you say if you could?[1]

purplish, every one
      a fine, thick
              rose
and all the following

        along the rivers
   Curages
          smell like honey

    plenty

   to the bees

---

[1] Language excerpted from *Florula Ludoviciana*, entry for Smartweed. Title taken from Bhanu Kapil's questions in *The Vertical Interrogration of Strangers*.

Four Poems

Sarah Mangold

Exchange Of Flowers And Signs

I was by nature averse to classification and counting.
She had already suspected passionate divination.
Scientific illustration as mere notion. Her theory of
plant metamorphosis might be incommunicable.
Women and plants alike. Flower momentarily entering
the realm of history and speech.

A Stretch Is Far More Serious Than A Cut

One good stomach and a clear head. My highly feminized agency. Plant Explorers and other hunger fighters. A picture cannot be the same at all hours of the day. To look wild to the most indifferent observer.

How To Preserve And Manage Joy

in papers

flesh shown

drown

diseases past

diseases we now rarely

an intelligible account

of the first few hundred

kinds of flowers

other flowers

other beetles

Object Of Its Own Index

Skin disrupts the distance   Undoes possible author functions
        Understand them both as leaving
Given all mistakes and idiosyncrasies of its manufacture
        Skin is the trace
                An outer marking of an internal structure
Begin to reveal yourself   Creature in landscape
A copy of that which cannot properly be said to exist

Preface to *Incapacity*

Jeanne Heuving

A few decades ago the desire to write a kuntslerroman announced itself to me with all the compulsion and vagueness for which I listen. This desire was connected to a previous piece of writing on which I had worked intermittently for several years and yielded these lines:

> In beginning the piece she first thought about writing one morning while living the uneventful events of that morning she had decided in advance to write about, she could not decide between herself as the main protagonist or someone like her. In thinking about herself as the protagonist, her sense of character disappeared as she did not experience herself in any coherent way, and in thinking of someone like her, her sense of events disappeared, as nothing so eventful had occurred as her desire to write just this piece. Certainly, she reasoned, someone like her could also desire to write this piece, but once she formulated her desire in this way, it would disappear into the confines of her writing and she would have no desire to write it.

From this conundrum came the thought that I would write *Jeanne* through compiling writing I had written before I thought to write this work. Since I had always written from the perspective of myself, whether in journals, traditional stories, or experimental pieces, I reasoned that I was embedded in this work in ways that I could not through any retrospective vantage possibly access. It was precisely in the revealing lapses of this writing, even in what some might consider awkward or bad writing, that in fact I was most present. Was not the ineptness, the incapacity of this writing, far more me than any overreaching understanding that would cover over the entity, myself, inserted into a narrative that in assuming knowledge of an unknown me all but eclipsed me.

Even though I felt quite committed to writing *Jeanne*, I feared that my idea for it was rather belated. Hadn't Andy Warhol already done the experiment of *cinema verite ad nauseum,* beginning with *Sleep* and filming his friend while he slept for five hours. Then John Ashbery in *Three Poems* had concluded that no solution was to be had in either putting everything in or taking everything out. I wondered in compiling this very long document *Jeanne* who would want to read through all its writing to break open the shell and discover the real Jeanne who had no particular hold over anyone's imagination except perhaps Jeanne herself and a few friends.

Nevertheless, I persisted, and selected and arranged into sections an exhaustive array of my writings. There were pieces written from the perspective of "I," "she," "we," and Jeannette, Ramona, Sylvia. Over time, I xeroxed and bound at Kinko's versions of *Jeanne*, also called *A Virginal, Snowball, and Enigmatic Variations*, all with velo binding and the same gray and white vinyl cover that was meant to imitate marble but for me stood for white skies with gray clouds. In compiling this work, I had the thought that I would somehow discover and transform myself such that my conundrums would create me rather than stopping me in my tracks. In order to conclude *Jeanne*, I would write a series of letters to well known writers, in order to actualize the passage of Jeanne into the world of letters. How better to conclude this book and its vague inclinations through situating myself in the world at large by writing letters to writers who spoke to me and with whom I wished to speak. I would through the writing and publication of these letters enact my movement into a public realm and literalize the concept of the public in the publication itself.

Through various transformations, *Jeanne* became *Incapacity*, and it was through this nomination that I discovered

the virtue of that which is formally differentiating. *Incapacity* was
a second stage reading and writing of the work I had completed
in *Jeanne*. In the first stages of *Jeanne*, even slight authorial
altercations of my previous writing had been quite forbidden. But it
was in the shaping of my manuscript and deletion of a great number
of pages that I began to discover both Jeanne and a readable book.
As I came to remake *Jeanne* as *Incapacity*, I felt far closer to Jeanne
than I had previously in the compilation of this document. This was
Jeanne in process or the event of Jeanne given form.

    Incapacity named a manifold incapacity, not only in the
protagonist herself but in the very act of inscription. Incapacity was
already well inscribed in the book as subject matter and the word
"incapacity" had surfaced repeatedly in my preceding writings, often
with respect to the set of questions of what did any one piece of
writing hold and how did it hold it. At times, incapacity had taken on
mysterious dimensions, as if it held the key to my being:

> Why when I seem so able in person and in thinking, am I
> so incapable? What kind of passivity is there in me that I
> should always feel I cannot simply apply myself or things
> to myself? Of course I secretly commend myself for some
> integrity which refuses to articulate anything when so much
> of me would remain inactivated by the articulation. I am
> rather excited by how I have seem to have overflowed
> certain boundaries. The other night in bed I felt quite
> hopeless. What I had long held off was now happening to
> me and I could do nothing about it. There would be much
> pain but some awful deadness was now gone. So much
> deadness in myself and incapacity. I am drawn to the word
> incapacity, all it cannot hold.

    Through this act of naming, I not only began deleting pre-
existing writing but also creating new writing for *Incapacity*. I came to
understand the book as composed of two different kinds of writing,
writing that stayed very close to the everyday realities of my life and
writing that took on distinctly literary domains. The quotidian writing
included journal entries that I replicated verbatim as well as a writing
meant to be coincident with my life as I was living it. The latter was
impossible given the difference between living and writing, but I
broached these by having my present include the activity of writing
itself:

She came across the idea of writing a story that began enshrouded in mist, while leafing through old notebooks one summer morning enshrouded in mist. Now that she had gotten the idea out in the open, it could serve as a misty enclosure that would make writing pleasurable, something far kinder than any life outside of it. How outside of her she had been by trying to be too much inside it. Only by viewing the inside of her life from the outside could she begin to effect the casual attitude she sometimes possessed in living, but rarely managed in writing.

In this writing, I came to realize that I need not only stay with the events in my life but I could also include writing I was reading. I began with Dorothy Sayers' *Gaudy Night*, as a friend had given me this book for my birthday and I liked the title, and then added to it books which had importance in my pantheon of reading. I made lists of sentences that I liked from these books and began rewriting these as they crossed into my life as I was living it and into the writing I had already written. Now I was writing my own present through appropriation, although at the time neither the concept nor the practice had yet announced itself, or at least not to me. In addition to *Gaudy Night*, I imported sentences from Emily Bronte's *Wuthering Heights* and Marguerite Duras's *The Ravishing of Lol V. Stein*. In grafting my writing to these writings, I came to accept the fictional nature of all formulation and also came to understand these formulations as partial truths in an onward moving, mutating existence. These articulations enhanced my life by allowing me to feel what was incipient in my life and gave it dimension and beauty through the empowered words of others. I could enrich my threadbare preoccupations through borrowing and rewording:

She, who does not see herself, is thus seen in others. She is erecting a scaffolding, which it would appear, is temporarily necessary for her, a woods, a field of wheat, a patience . . . She freezes because of something going on inside her, what?, unknown, savage leitmotifs, swilling rose petals, cracked newspaper glass. The heat of summer which till that day she had listlessly endured explodes and spreads. She is submerged in it. Everything is: the street, the town, this stranger.

In order to publish *Incapacity*, I needed to end the book, and so would necessarily compromise its main concept; it would become a capacity. In order to mitigate this effect, I thought to include photographs. This change of media would disrupt any premature closure, any willing suspension of disbelief that might have accrued through the accumulated aspects of the piece. As visual documents they demanded a different mode of apprehension and so the reader would be jarred from any sense that *Incapacity* had been concluded. There were bleak photographs, of the back yard where I had grown up, ivy covering the rockery that divided our house from the house behind us and a slab of concrete that we called the patio, and of melting snow on the street where I now lived. Then, there were distant worlds, of the cones of volcanoes circling Lake Atitlan and of a collapsed hillside in Guatemala City after an earthquake, and of San Francisco after an earthquake there.

In 2004, I published *Incapacity*, although it did not hold all of my ambitions for *Jeanne*. I have added two new books to *Incapacity*, *Inconsolate* and *Correspondence*. In many ways *Inconsolate* is a palimpsest of the already palimpsestic *Incapacity*. All of the pieces in *Inconsolate*, including additional Daybooks sections, were written before I thought to write *Jeanne* and are focused on houses and rooms, as if the protagonist seeks some enclosure, some limited capacity, at the expense of situating herself in the world. Written at a time before the internet and social media electrified social relations, the spaces of the pieces seem surprisingly pedestrian and quiet. And while I then lived amongst people for whom Marxist politics and women's consciousness raising were part of our daily conversation, I did not feel that I could incorporate these ideas into what I then called "my writing" without giving a lie to the actual life I was living. It was as if my writing to be my writing must elect limited vantages, glimpsed worlds, leaving me locked into spaces, sometimes as my solitary self and sometimes as a dyadic couple. For if in fact the protagonist seems peculiarly alone and incapable of change, the relationships she finds herself in seem to be similarly isolated islands of human inaction.

In these pieces I write as if aware of these limitations, but as if adhering to these restrictions promises me some movement forward, what the protagonist euphemistically refers to as her "personal development." But while I seem in search of some kind of personal transformation, I expend myself in describing physical interiors. In the section of "Houses" titled "Hotel Universe," the name of a group house where I lived, I go against the rules of the house which maintained a policy of never locking its doors so that friends, or whomever, could find refuge in the house when they wished, by installing locks on my bedroom door:

> In moving into the house, I made my bedroom the center of my existence, in what had been a den or second parlor on the first floor. There were two entrances to my room, one through the double mahogany doors off the entrance vestibule and another by way of a long circuitous route through the kitchen and a hidden hallway. In order to have privacy, I always used the back entrance, keeping the double mahogany doors permanently shut. On the inside of both doorways, I installed manual hooks and eyes so that I could lock myself in. In screwing the bolts into the doors and watching the fresh wood surface from beneath the dark, stained lacquered wood, I felt pleasantly outside of the house's rules. Not only was I finding a way of protecting myself, but I was going against the household rules, that no further damage, or change, should be inflicted on the house's original features—namely the yellowing wallpaper and the mahogany wood. While I did feel bad about damaging the mahogany wood, I was quite convinced that my own needs superseded these rules and no one would ever know that I had broken the house rules— except if they trespassed into my room.

In "Elegiac Stanzas," in the first section called "Beach Scene," I write out of a sense of physical obstruction and frustrated movement. In this piece, the protagonist and her boyfriend vacation in a down-in-the-heels beach resort and town. The piece begins with how this couple in not managing to live together seek out vacation places where they might share the same abode:

> In the several years we were together we never managed to live together, so our vacations had to make up for a lot of indecision and loneliness. We were always trying to find the perfect place where we could exist in something resembling conjugal happiness. We would trade off certain

attributes for others. For instance, if there was a fireplace, we would relinquish our desires for a swimming pool, and vice versa. For a while we were determined to stay in fifties motels on little traveled highways, with swimming pools in the shape of natural lakes and ponds. But wherever we stayed, we always isolated a certain quality or feature that recommended it for our unique use.

Arriving at Rock-A-Way Resort on Rock-A-Way Beach, they find themselves amidst much physical dereliction not only in their cabin itself but in the town of Rock-A-Way. They try to make the cabin over to reflect themselves, throwing the synthetic pink bed cover with its fraying roses into the closet and covering the torn couch with a blanket they had intended for the beach. Yet, the sense of physical dereliction persists not only in this cabin but in the beach town where they find they can only proceed with difficulty "over the cracked, moss-lined sidewalks with their skate boards and dolls, never quite making it to the end of the town, to the gas station that was also a restaurant and the hardware store which sold maternity wear." The piece concludes with the announcement of the demise of this relationship and the statement, "When I seek the reasons for our break up, I can understand how the whole thing quit working one day. But when I think of the actual events, I am not certain how any one thing ever passes into the next." In the second section, "Divided Lights," I replicate passages from two stories, Chekov's "Enemies" and Flannery O'Conner's "The Artificial Negro," contemplating the desire to move forward, although as the wayfarers "walk and walk" "the ground they walk on is always the same . . . the spot remains a spot."

Inconsolate ends with "Poetic Justice." In the piece called "Seduction," the narrator contemplates a grade school seduction scene between herself and her boyfriend, and she witnesses death from a glassed-in hospital observing room, a death which she eventually comes to realize is her own, as the blue of her iris spills into a surrounding blue lake. In "The High Bridge Above the / Tagus River at Toledo," I imitate the syntax and rhythms of William Carlos Wiliams' poem of the same title, in order to walk forward, and eventually toward a city that appears out of the gloaming. Even so, the piece concludes that while she was "approaching the generous possibilities of a novel," "Never would there be anything so lovely as a city at nightfall . . . . Only retrospectively would the city emerge, a mirage she had already passed through."

I conclude *Incapacity* with *Correspondence* which consists of additional Daybooks and sequences of letters. While a failed sense of mimesis and mirroring relations subtend *Incapacity*, the pieces in *Correspondence* address these impulses while not foreclosing on the inevitable gaps between oneself and others in our lives or a lived life and writing. I take some measure from both Walter Benjamin and Jacques Lacan. Walter Benjamin in "The Faculty of Mimesis" insists on mimesis as an impulse rather than a product. For Benjamin, "nonsensuous similarity" occurs as a flash of recognition, and it is through "the coherence of words and sentences" that similarity is experienced. He notes: "It is not improbable that the rapidity of writing and reading heightens the fusion of the semiotic and the mimetic in the sphere of language."

Lacan in "The Mirror Stage," although intent on the misrecognition of mirroring relations, also notes their generative aspect:

> That a Gestalt should be capable of formative effects in the organism is attested by a piece of biological experimentation that is itself so alien to the idea of psychical causality that it cannot bring itself to formulate its results in these terms. It nevertheless recognizes that it is a necessary condition for the maturation of the gonad of the female pigeon that it should see another member of its species, of either sex; so sufficient in itself is this condition that the desired effect may be obtained merely by placing the individual within reach of the field of reflection of a mirror.
>
> . . . .
>
> Similarly, in the case of the migratory locust, the transition within a generation from the solitary to the gregarious form can be obtained by exposing the individual, at a certain stage, to the exclusively visual action of a similar image, provided it is animated by movements of a style sufficiently close to that characteristic of the species. Such facts are inscribed in an order of homeomorphic identification that would itself fall within the larger question of the meaning of beauty as both formative and erogenic.

In *Correspondence*, the Daybooks pieces are structured around mirroring opposites. In one Daybooks piece, I tell of an incident when I was a child and climbed up on the mantel over our fireplace in order to try to enter the mirror that hung there and so experience what it felt to live in the life over there. In the section called simply "Letters," I include several of the letters I first wrote for *Jeanne*, letters to James, Wayne Koestenbaum, Kathleen Fraser, and Helene Cixous. The manner of writing is baroque or fugue-like with statements appearing in one letter recurring in later letters. The pieces both concern questions about writing and the vicissitudes of every day life. I write to Kathleen Fraser about her sense of importance of a "loose voice" and of sitting in a café with James, my helpmeet, who having injured his fingers in a power saw accident, began telling stories of musicians who had hurt their hands that later healed so they could play their instruments as before:

> I was trying to think loosely of a different way of writing, recalling your 'the loose voice, no less, is crucial,' when James, his two fingers chewed by his table saw, began telling peculiar stories of musicians with major careers who hurt their hands, which later came to heal so that they could play again. I was surprised by the stories that James was telling of hurt hands reunited with musical instruments, since in his change of careers from classical music to furniture making, James had not been inclined toward stories of joyous reunions with musical instruments, but rather of anger at the demands of classical preservation. The whole morning seemed a haven from the terrible danger that rushed us to the emergency room, as he now sat with stinging fingers wrapped in bandages that will most likely heal well enough so that he will be able to push twisted hard metals through his table saw and play his lithesome guitar as before.

These letters are followed by a sequence of letters to "Dear Miss Lonelyhearts," written to the fictional character in Nathanael West's *Miss Lonelyhearts*, a newspaper man who writes a lonely hearts column under the guise of Miss Lonelyhearts. These letters trammel the circumspection of the preceding letters, as the careful address of the preceding letters give way to heart throb. Not only does Shell Shocked as she sometimes calls herself beseech Miss Lonelyhearts for love but also for writing instruction. She implores him and then quotes directly from Nathanael West:

I sense you would rather sleep curled like an embryo into a cerulean blue than to write me a letter. Then I am thinking of going out in my little rowboat, water lapping at the bottom. A cat suckling milk from a woman's exposed nipples on the cantilevered steps of sculpture park on an August evening in Rome. Should you write or never, exhuming ghost. *As a boy in his father's church, he had discovered that something stirred in him when he shouted the name of Christ, something secret and enormously powerful. He knew now what this thing was, a snake whose scales are tiny mirrors in which the dead world takes on semblances of life. Love a man even in his sin, for that is the semblance of Divine Love. Love all God's creation, the whole and every grain of sand in it. If you love everything, you will perceive the divine mystery of things.*

I end *Correspondence* with "Translation," a compilation of passages from letters between Antonin Artaud and Jacques Ranciere. I came across these letters shortly after publishing the first *Incapacity*. At the time they seemed so replete, so evocative, of everything I had attempted in Incapacity that this flash of recognition makes them a suitable conclusion to my newly minted Incapacity. In these letters a youthful Artaud attempts to enlist Ranciere's attention to his literary works, and refuses that their value should be reduced because of what he admits is their failed execution. I do not distinguish between Artaud and Ranciere in the letters as the two letters together strike me as a compilation of the difficulties and solutions I had sought for my own writing: "It is very important that the few manifestations of *spiritual* existence that I have been able to give myself not be regarded as inexistent because of the blotches and awkward expressions with which they are marred." "One thing that strikes me: the contrast between the extraordinary precision of your self-diagnosis and the vagueness, or at least formlessness of what you are endeavoring to achieve. . . . To put it more precisely, this is how I see the matter: the mind is fragile in that it needs obstacles-adventitious obstacles. If it is alone, it loses its way, it destroys itself. . . . ". "There is no absolute peril except for him who abandons himself."

The Taste of Elsewhere:
love and iodine in
the writing of Stacey Levine

John Olson

Stacey Levine has a keen sense of elsewhere. Elsewhere is an important place. I know it's an important place because André Breton, who was an expert on elsewhere, ended his *Manifesto of Surrealism* with this important reference to elsewhere: "It is living and ceasing to live that are imaginary solutions. Existence is elsewhere."

I sensed this quality immediately when I first began reading Stacey Levine. Her drollery, her exquisite sense of the absurd, were imbued with a wistful sadness. The awkwardness of life, its stigmas and wounds, its inflammations and scars, its natural comedy and inherent sadness were all combined in a prose style that felt relaxed and ingenuous while simultaneously expressing something very exotic or macabre. The gentle fluidity of her sentences would often present a unique, unorthodox perspective or quirky detail that was all the more penetrating because of the subtlety in which it was embedded. It was positively enchanting. The ineffable - that chimera that haunts all truly compelling work - pulsed in her words with a quiet tremor. It reminded me a great deal of the paintings by Henri Rousseau, those innocently rendered jungle scenes in which wild animals peer out through the foliage with bright, wide-eyed bemusement.

My introduction to Stacey's writing began with a novel titled *Frances Johnson*. How can you not like a book named *Frances Johnson?*

Frances Johnson is the story of a woman who wants to be elsewhere. She lives in a town in Florida called Munson, which adjoins Little Munson. Some few miles distant in the ocean is an active volcano. Frances has a partner named Ray, with whom she enjoys certain intimacies, but there is no romance or sexuality. There may be romance and sexuality. But if they exist, they exist quietly in another story. Or noisily in another story. *Frances Johnson* is focused on the quiet inner dramas of our life, the conflicts we wrestle with privately. Sex and romance have a gauzy ambiguity here in these pages. There is sometimes a kiss that comes into focus but full-on sexual intimacy is somewhere out there in the haze with the volcano. The agitations at the core of this book are only indirectly linked with romance. Something more transcendent seems to be urging the central character to get out, move on, do something. The symptoms aren't hormonal. They're otherworldly. They're representative of a stubborn pathology, an unresolved yearning to be elsewhere. Frances wants out. Just out. Anywhere. But can't. Some indefinable force keeps her trapped in Munson, encumbers her like the mud that frequently cakes to her bicycle wheels.

I know this feeling. I feel it most acutely when I experience a strange phenomenon called "sleep paralysis." It's not at all like the sleep I experience when I go to bed, but happens when I nod off while reading, or staring at the ceiling. I'll be dreaming that I'm under attack, being chased by a monster, a swarm of angry wasps, a giant orange-colored man-baby with bright blonde Aryan hair and a smirk coming at me with a baseball bat, but I can't move. I need to get up. I need to take action. But I can't. I'm paralyzed. And the odd thing about it is that it occurs when I begin to wake up, just seconds before I attain full consciousness. Scientists aren't sure what it is, but think it might be linked to post-synaptic inhibition in the pons, or back region of the brain. Whatever it is, I know what it feels like to yearn to be elsewhere, to be completely fed up with myself and life on this planet, and want out of this existence. "Let us flee to lands that are analogues of death," Baudelaire intones in a prose poem titled "Anywhere Out Of This World." He suggests a number of travel possibilities to his soul. "At last my soul explodes, and wisely cries out to me: 'no matter where! No matter where! As long as it's out of the world!'"

Frances visits a physician named Palmer. She is worried about a scar on her leg, a "clumpy mass of tissue on her thigh." "The scar actually seemed to be formed of clusters of smaller scars bearing a resemblance to boils, and dried, black blood lined its crevices." The scar persists. It is not mentioned what caused the injury in the first place, but the scar, like all scars, assumes a significance not unlike the narrative compaction of a tattoo. Some people are proud of their scars. This is not one of those instances. The scar is an outward manifestation of an inner turmoil. There are numerous other instances in *Frances Johnson* in which a certain persistent detail pulls the attention deeper into the words and vibrates like the harmonic on a wind-blown bridge. It's a haunting effect, and can be something as quietly effective in its pathos as a man tripping over a stick, "his mouth an open circle below the glasses tumbling from his eyes."

It has been a number of years since I first read *Frances Johnson*, which was published in 2005. I've read other work by Stacey as well, and have enjoyed the privilege of knowing her and hearing her read. I have often felt a certain comradeship with her. We share a taste for the droll, the macabre, and the prevailing weirdness of life in general. She struck me as comedic at first, funny in the way that Eugene Ionesco is funny, that theatre of the absurd sensibility that seeps into you like nitrous oxide and makes you feel like you've stepped into a cartoon panel, all your dialogue above your head in balloons. She is a little bit of that, but I think droll is a better word. There is a wistful, bittersweet quality to her writing, a dreamy melancholy imbuing what at first sounds simply comic. Nothing, of course, is ever simply comic, but there is a significant difference between what is ludicrous and what is peculiar. A good *Saturday Night Live* skit is not the same as *Waiting for Godot*. One is parody, the other is starkly absurd. Death is never mentioned in *Garfield* or *Dagwood*, but you can hear its woeful rustlings in the lawns and curtains of Stacey's words.

A very recent piece of fiction by Stacey that appeared in *The Brooklyn Rail* called "Brown Seaweed Soup" happily moved within my orbit. I'm a big fan of soup, and while my feelings about seaweed are generally neutral, it only seems natural that it might be an ingredient in soup cooked up by my friend Stacey Levine. "Brown seaweed soup," she begins,

> is a kind of a soup with brown seaweed in it. Brown seaweed soup is an important food as well as a healing medicine. With its profusion of ferrous iodine, brown seaweed soup surpasses other soups and can reanimate women after childbirth. A cleaner of blood vessels, this soup has become synonymous not only with health and birthdays, but with painful, vital hindsight.

Hindsight, they say, is 20 20. This is true. This is what makes it painful. You can see everything clearly once it's happened. You can see how things went wrong, how things that were said could hurt, how you might've modified your response to a situation, been a little cooler, a little more detached, a little more measured and balanced. But that's not how life works. When you're in the moment, you don't have lines. Nothing has been scripted for you. You're on your own. Spontaneity and impulse have their own kinds of beauty and reality, but they're not typos you can later proofread and discard. You're stuck with them. They acquire a flavor. Hindsight has a flavor. It's full of iron, and remorse, and tastes a lot like seaweed.

Stacey's story concerns a man named Bruce, who has disappeared. He has died. He is gone. And this is ultimately what much of life is about: loss.

Loss is bitter. It can crush you.

Sometimes something can die in you and leave you in life still standing, doing dishes, gazing mournfully out of a kitchen window. There is that kind of death. It's not a real death. Real death is indescribable. It's an absolute so final it's breath-taking. You can throw as many words as you can at it and it's still going to stand there, black and deep and unfathomable. Nothing you say or write is going to change it. There is something sublime about it. It's unequivocal. Totally non-negotiable. Look what happened to Orpheus. He gave it a shot. Didn't work out.

Bruce's father, a mathematician, brings the family to the Cote d'Ivoire where he teaches introductory calculus to a sugar baron. Yanked out of his life, Bruce becomes a lost, mournful figure.

"With his now-dead eyes, Bruce as a child watched the tall standup boulders off the coast, the lacquered Atlantic gulf ankling him to the sand."

What a marvelous sentence that is. "Ankling" sounds a lot like anchor, and so the image delivers a sensation of weight, rootedness, and the shine of oblivion. The lacquer of loss. The varnish of the indifferent.

As a grown man, Bruce finds his way to Paris, where he continually gets lost, a problem he solves by going to the Gare du Nord and catching a train to Madrid.

Bruce gets around.

A few paragraphs later and we find Bruce studying tree phloem in Petaluma, California, and living in a "scrunty tent."

Then Berlin. I won't reveal further what happens to Bruce and so spoil the story for those who have not yet had a sip of this engaging concoction, but bow away gracefully, waiting for that flavor, that salty, bittersweet taste of seaweed to imbue my palate. The taste of hindsight. "Painful, vital hindsight."

Is hindsight good for us? Does it contain vitamins? Vitamin C? Vitamin D?

C for crouton. Crustacean. Courage.

D for depot. Detail. Daydream.

Roland Barthes, drawing on Georges Bataille, talks about an amorous rhythm between knowledge and value. *Le savoir, le valeur.* They interact, balance one another. This puzzles me. Isn't knowledge a value to begin with? Or is he suggesting that knowledge can sometimes be worthless?

Knowledge is inherently valuable because, even as a polemic that has gone wrong or overcomplicates things, it is an antidote to boredom, to ennui, to that feeling of emptiness that dogs everyone's heels.

Fiction is very much the same. I find this quality to an acute degree in Stacey's writing.

She is very specific about the kind of seaweed to use for this soup: laver. It is a Welsh word, where a traditional dish called laverbread is made. The seaweed is a littoral alga. It is smooth in texture and forms an undifferentiated glop of organic material high in iodine and iron, and is quite often found clinging to coastal rocks.

Like hindsight. Hindsight is high in iron and clings to the

back of my brain. That's why it's called hindsight. I see my life in a
rearview mirror, a camera obscura like the one it is theorized that
Vermeer used for his paintings. The camera obscura is essentially
a converging lens and a viewing screen at the opposite end of the
darkened chamber. The images assume a striking clarity, although
they have been separated from the real world, and are now
dreamlike apparitions cast on a wall.

Is language violent? It surely can be. It propagates madly,
crazily, like nothing else on the surface of this planet. Language
has a lot in common with seaweed. Its iron can be hammered into
swords, riveted into tanks, or mingled into the blood for vitality. It
has a bittersweet taste. Crafted into a story by Stacey Levine, it can
sound intensely mournful, a little bizarre, a little nutty, and powerfully,
subtly intense, like Willie Dixon and Koko Taylor singing "Insane
Asylum."

"When your love has ceased to be (Lord have mercy),
there's no other place for me."

The Camel's Pedestal
by Anne Tardos

Jeanne Heuving

The Camel's Pedestal veers between thought articulated so
specifically there is no room for further thought, of thought agitating
in the aporia of thought, and of thought giving up on itself, relaxing
into play and splay. This is a work composed of lines and bears out
Rachel DuPlessis's remark on Tardos's earlier *Nine* (2015), "the
lines are each porous in relation to each other." But whereas in *Nine,*
a procedure of nine is followed, as Tardos explains in an opening
poem, "nine words per line and nine lines per stanza," *The Camel's
Pedestal* (2017), as the title indicates, is more eccentric. There are
somewhat lengthy serial poems and short one-pagers; lines that are
complete sentences and lines that are phrases, long lines and short
lines.

The work moves gracefully whether making a point or
absconding with sense-making. Often these two are engaged within
the same poem so as to initiate, engage, and blur the ways that any
one thought might take an upper hand. As Tardos writes. "She works
'by reason of making,' wishing to extend what she already knows."
She asserts, "The right to rummage through all that I see and hear."

About a third of the book is made up by poems paired
on opposing pages that demonstrate the variability inherent in

opposition itself. Take, for instance, "Clear" and "The Noble Lie," a seeming opposition that through Tardos's pen becomes a cascading set of relations that trip each other up. "Clear" at once manifests a clear desire for clarity, such that one not only understands the desire for this standard but also feels it, as in "Seeking pleasure is clear." Yet the very propensity to seek "clear" also produces a clear that hardens and delimits, given its controlling demand: "calling all of it clear is also clear." Here, then the word "clear" manifests its arbitrary imposition on a more fluid order of things, as clear vacillates, at once opaque and transparent. This is not at all clear. The poem then turns from this investigation to offer a series of clear and unclear oppositions. There is "Carbon copy. Dulcimer" and "Ropes around my mouth and rosemary-flavored lollipops."

The poem on the opposing page, "The Noble Lie," creates involved propositions that if not exactly truths, and certainly not clear truths, provide motivation to stay with these, to dwell amongst these assertions, as in "The cognitive value of happiness and well-being function as endless enjoyment." And "Carefully crafted pathways lead to unknown places where longing leaves hesitation behind."

"Clear" and "The Noble Lie" are in a face-off demonstration of their delimiting linguistic and cognitive make-up. This is not a clear opposition, as one might think abstractly in considering the two titles, but rather poems that are neighborly, desirous perhaps, or not, of some kind of fence between them. (One is reminded of the double meaning of fence, to serve as a barrier or to deal in stolen goods.) "Clear" is in many ways about the dictates of a word; whereas "The Noble Lie" takes on formation.

While much of *The Camel's Pedestal* is thought contending with thought, there are other valences and tones, as in "Tenderness in Late Afternoon Light." Tardo writes, "A certain preparation of mind, where tenderness in late afternoon light sits at the edge of a chair. // Takes my breath away." At times Tardos summarizes, refusing the pitch of poetry, as if routine experience with its own platitudinous expanse is best spoken through deflationary rhetoric: "I see many paths to a better life, many routines to engage in, voices to listen to, admired ones to imitate, parks to visit, animals to comfort, words to invent , phrases to think of lives to improve, routines to follow, friends to invite over, temptations to resist, sounds to get used to or annoyed at—there is no shortage of things to do on the path to a better life."

Tardos is described in the brief biography that informs this book as having "pioneered a unique multilingual writing style, often complementing her texts with video stills, photographs, and collages." Yet, in this exclusively print book, a stillness pervades, not only because it does not engage "multiple languages" and diverse media, but because social context is rarely elicited. Social context, of course, enters into poetry through many means, sometimes through overt statements that conjure particular social contexts, but often through language itself, that as social idiolect inevitably produces traces of the social through its tonalities, syntax, and connotations.

Although the first poem in the book, clearly stakes out social existence—the only poem to do so—"The Enigma of Being Jewish" is much more compelled by the enigma of identity than being Jewish per se, except perhaps to suggest that Jewishness inheres in enigma itself. While the poem makes a few direct allusions to actual Jews, namely Derrida and Cixous, much of the poem lists characteristics that in their generalities could also be about many peoples: "We produce texts. Think about what to write. We implement and follow diversity policies." Indeed one line enjoins us to ignore the title: "Never mind the titles. They can be anything you like." Another line declares: "Gender neutral, one is free to speak to unspeakable."

This election of a writing that flaunts specific social identities or relations is part of what this book is about. I am reminded of Laura (Riding) Jackson, who objected to a writing in which individuals would define themselves in relationship to a compromising social order, what she called "an individual real," opting instead for "an individual unreal," albeit Tardos, in general, takes on a much more exploratory relation to things as they are, in contrast to the often defiant (Riding) Jackson.

While in other works Tardos is multilingual, she seems to have adopted here something of a lingua franca, a direction pursued by others at this time. I am thinking, for instance, of the lingua franca of Chris Kraus's biography, *After Kathy Acker*, that is very much "after" Acker, given its clearly written, declarative style, and contrasts with Acker's own modalities, who once wrote, "I was unspeakable so I ran into the language of others." Or more generally, the direction taken currently by many poets and intellectuals in order to create a speech more accessible to more people, and an actionable politics.

I miss in *The Camel's Pedestal*, the expanse and diversity of heard speech, as in Susan Howe's sense of poems in *The Midnight* as "the impossibility of plainness rendered in plainest form." Or in Mei Mei Bersenbrugge's "Hearing": "She's not speaking words I hear in an undertone" or "My hearing touches my limit on all sides, a community exposed."

While the turn to lingua franca is meant to gather audiences put off by the difficulty of preceding writing, or perhaps in Tardos case to delimit the over-determination of the social itself, it quiets social noise. Yet the promise of poetry and language are their explosive limitations.

Anne, Tardos, *The Camel's Pedestal: Poems 2009-2017*. BlazeVOX [books]. Buffalo, NY: 2017. 101 pp.

That Dionysian Jazz

Amy L. Friedman

A lone figure sits on a stump. This is the cover image of Rochelle Owens's newest poetry volume, Hermaphropoetics, Drifting Geometries. With slightly downcast shoulders and a pensive air, it could be Estragon, or Vladimir. It is, in fact, an image titled "Person Who Is Sitting On A Tree Stump," and as the first thing encountered as an introduction to a long poem which relentlessly challenges the categories of gender and sex, notions of ontology, and the expectations of linear narrative, the image is apt.

Work by Rochelle Owens should bring to mind an instant association with groundbreaking writing, if one has seen or read her Off-Off-Broadway plays such as Futz and Istanboul or read her book-length poems. She should be immediately tagged as an avant-garde artist, one who challenges, reinvents, innovates. A long time ago, in 1981, Rochelle Owens was asked to create a writer's statement to contribute to a collection of manifestos about the arrival of a new poetics. She wrote memorably and incisively: "Because I am bored by the traditional, conventionalized and fossilized systems of writing poetry and plays, they are useless, I demolish them." It is not surprising that critic and scholar Tim Good refers to her as a revolutionary. I rather think she should be commissioned as a demolitions expert, first-class.

At the time Rochelle Owens began publishing her poetry in Diane Di Prima and LeRoi Jones's Greenwich Village journal, Yugen, cultural observers elsewhere were noting, sometimes tepidly, that literary journals and performances were breaking boundaries, and reflecting a degree of innovative change in the fringe arts scene. But Owens was never interested in anything as milquetoast as mere "change." Her fearless focus was always on driving the cutting edge, and on the avant garde as something that shapes its own reality.

It is justified to find in Owens's Hermaphropoetics some echoes of her powerful earlier epic book-length poetic works, The Joe 82 Creation Poems (1974) and The Joe Chronicles Part 2 (1979). In these works Owens is investigating a gender-undermining approach to language, which in Hermaphropoetics becomes a front-and-center concentration on a principal hermaphroditic figure, for whom gendered language is split, hyphenated, and augmented. In the earlier work, The Joe 82 Creation Poems, there is a major figure, the Wild-woman, adjacent to the poem's Wild-man; these two are at times in tense juxtaposition. The Wild-woman possesses paradoxically "masculine" traits which nonetheless enable her to flourish. The Wild-woman is resilient, imaginative, assured, sexual, and energetic, and at one point she names herself a "Woman-Abraham," empowered to establish a cult, to inspire followers, to make an impact, as a leader who pronounces on rites of naming and creation.

Hermaphropoetics in some ways continues these lines of investigation, but in a markedly different and singular way; the masculine and feminine have now totally fused. More arguably happens and has happened in this long poem than in the Joe poems, but less is explained.

Hermaphropoetics is a work of experimental and ethnopoetic practice, crafted in short, repetitive strophes; each strophe is but one, two or three taut lines. The text repeats an overarching narrative of an isolated figure, stump-seated. Dramatic events have

taken place. The scene is perhaps being filmed, and in the poem a
camera takes pictures, and whole sections of the work are named as
both elements of geometry and cinematography: "Angle," "Focus,"
"Spiral," "Zoom." The camera angles suggest shifting perspectives
as well as the poet's term, "Shifting Geometries." Violent things have
happened, but a tide of phrases of fecundity nonetheless throbs
throughout.

> a hermaphrodite
> captured after the siege
>
> a hermaphrodite
> emptied of allegory
>
> seated on the stump of a tree
>
> his soaring paper thin
> shoulderblades
>
> The master photographer
> focuses the lens
>
> The camera zooms and pans
>
> the dome of her skull
> his earlobes...
>
> his legs collapsing under her
> his mouth waters   taste buds pulsate
>
> a flow of hormonal forces
>
> hypermasculine hyperfeminine
> murderous sex cells

    In the central action of ethnopoetics, a scribe respectfully
records the utterances which comprise the core of a culture. The
activity is intended to provide a record of performative aspects
of a cultural community, to preserve the order of words as they

are performed, and to note also the silences and the repetitions which might make a ritual utterance mystifying to a cultural outsider. Thus the chants of First Peoples can be inscribed without misrepresentation, and spared any inappropriate editing to impose a "neater," or euro-centric, or non-native, linear-narrative form. As an aesthetic, creative practice, ethnopoetics defies any imposed hierarchy of narrative line. Compulsory narrative may even be deemed suspect. And in Owens's Hermaphropoetics, we return inexplicably to the repeated narrative of the mysterious seated deaf-mute hermaphrodite, but as the figure seems more familiar as the text returns to his/her narrative, the descriptors shift and mutate. Sometimes it's "her platinum blond curls/bringing millions to their knees" and other times it's "his platinum blond curls/bringing millions to their knees," but always the power of the poetic line intensifies. Owens' writing in Hermaphropoetics has the weight of a national creation myth, or a projected future cultural originary story, with rhythmic phrases which, repeated, become choruses in celebration of a significant poetic mythos. But if that sounds in the least ponderous, then note with celerity the linguistic playfulness, the sharp imagery, and the wide-ranging, even mischievous cultural references which remind one that no poet writes for as many decades as Rochelle Owens has without also having fun.

> In this story
> ripening on the vine
>
> so to speak
>
> in this story
> a warhol-like playfulness
>
> a vinyl fruit of desire
>
> l'amore impossible   l'amour
> possible
>
> in a dream of a hermaphrodite
> in silhouette

her hollow bones
glow under a black light
magnetic his hollow bones

elegant the fusion of bird
and human

her soaring paper thin
shoulderblades

his sculpted pelvis

In the social psychology field of career construction theory, counselors ponder the stories that underpin how a professional career unfolds, to look at how an individual makes sense of the self-identity that evolves from an occupation. Transposed to the milieu of poets and playwrights, they might ponder what patterns and periods comprise the whole of a significant literary career, and how this impacts readers' judgements about individual works over time. An intriguing query develops about whether one might read "early" and "later" works by the same author in different ways, or with differing expectations of the gradations of "importance" that critics dole out when impacted positively by a work. Hywel Dix thinks about this a great deal in his recent monograph, The Late-Career Novelist: Career Construction Theory, Authors and Autofiction (Bloomsbury 2017), arguing "that whereas much critical attention has been devoted to establishing the idea of a major phase and hence to the transition between early and mature works of an author's career, the late stage has receive comparatively less attention." Dix's overall focus is on a "rigorous critical interrogation and provisional clarification" of what a "late" stage in an author's oeuvre might be discussed or construed as, and why. Dix takes issue with the way the idea of a "literary and artistic decline wrought by the process of aging" remains "common and hence unchallenged" in literary biographies, critical overviews, and retrospective writing about writers. He concludes that "to challenge the idea of distinct major and minor phases is also to challenge a cultural and social hierarchy based on age." Dix is accurate that there is a prevailing and quite dominant model, in which chronologically later work is expected to be a revisiting of a writer's prior themes and subjects, as if later work presupposes the exposition of the lifetime of worthy habits that the writer has engraved into the writing practice of a career; the successful artistic path is etched and then repeated. The assumption is that the distinguished writer, Dix continues, returns to techniques or forms for which he was celebrated, or she was recognized. The flaw in apprehensions of entire authorial careers is thus that there is little to no expectation of significant artistic development in work which is categorized as chronologically "late." And there is also scant appreciation, nor interpretive space allocated, for artistry which will never just follow on, but which will always veer anew.

Dix wants instead to interrogate any assumption of a "career high point and subsequent decline," and to assert instead that the way diverse stages of "a given authorial career are constructed" is in a manner which is simply specific to that career. Obvious, perhaps, but a stance which enables readers to divest expectation and to even read with a sense of suspense. The most crucial elements to alter in critical perceptions, according to Dix, are to bypass readings that seek "conformity" in a writer's output and to consider instead the criteria of "deviation and innovation." Edward Said put it another way in his posthumously published work, On Late Style: Music and Literature Against the Grain (2005), in a discussion about Theodor Adorno's comments on the ways in which Beethoven's final symphony, The Ninth Symphony, and final five piano sonatas convey both newness and "the irascible gesture" towards critical assumptions and expectations. Edward Said notes that regardless of our cognition of Beethoven's personal straits when he composed music in his later years, one can't reduce these later works "to the notion of art as a document" about his state of being, or to a reading of the musical material in which personal history "breaks through" and takes over. "Late style," Edward Said concludes, "is what happens if art does not abdicate its rights in favour of reality." Mature, fulfilled, deviant, innovative, and even irascible style is achieved when "late" is not acknowledged at all, as when the avant-garde artist continues to redefine his/her reality.

painterly images
cells forming cartilage

when the subatomic
particles when

when frame by frame
breakdown when

when burned
by its light source when

when at the edge
of the village when

when four bearded elders
circle when

when the bride holds
a mirror when

when she falls
to the ground when

when the village on fire
appears   disappears

With those deceptively straightforward, repeatedly deployed syllables of "when," the poet completely and efficiently disrupts the line. She embeds suspense and prompts silent readers to pronounce the poetry aloud, to lift the words from the pages, and to join her, Rochelle Owens, avant garde artist, in making that Dionysian jazz.

Rochelle Owens, Hermaphropoetics, Drifting Geometries, Singing Horse Press (San Diego, CA, 2017), $18.

Notes on Contributors

Rae Armantrout's most recent books, *Versed, Money Shot, Just Saying, Itself, Partly: New and Selected Poems,* and *Entanglements* (a chapbook selection of poems in conversation with physics), were published by Wesleyan University Press. In 2010 her book *Versed* won the Pulitzer Prize for Poetry and The National Book Critics Circle Award. *Wobble,* a new volume of her poems, is forthcoming from Wesleyan in September of 2018. She is recently retired from UC San Diego where she was professor of poetry and poetics. She currently lives in the Seattle area.

Amy L. Friedman is Assoc. Professor in Temple University's English Department, teaching many lit. courses including the Beat Generation, Women Modernists, and Satire. Her monograph, *Postcolonial Satire,* is upcoming from Lexington Press. She was an earlier scholar of women writers of the Beat Generation, and wrote about some of Rochelle Owens's early plays in *Beat Drama: Playwrights and Performances of the "Howl" Generation* (Methuen 2016).

Nancy Gaffield was born in the United States and has lived in England for many years. Her first book, *Tokaido Road* (CBe, 2011), won the Aldeburgh First Collection Prize and was shortlisted for the Forward First Collection Prize; an opera derived from *Tokaido Road* premiered in 2014. Her other poetry collections are *Continental Drift* (Shearsman, 2014), and three chapbooks. *Meridian* (forthcoming) follows the Greenwich Meridian line along public footpaths and bridleways from Sussex to the Humber in order to investigate the way that landscapes are disturbed and reordered by history and memory.

Alan Halsey's *Selected Poems 1988-2016* is published by Shearsman. He co-directs the antichoir Juxtavoices with Martin Archer; the group's latest release on Discus Records is the double CD/DVD *Warning: May Contain Notes*. He is an Affiliated Poet at Sheffield University's Centre for Poetry and Poetics.

Jeanne Heuving's *The Transmutation of Love and Avant-Garde Poetics* is recently out from the Modern and Contemporary Poetics series at the University of Alabama Press. Her cross genre book *Incapacity* (Chiasmus Press) won a 2004 Book of the Year Award from Small Press Traffic. Other books include *Transducer* (Chax), *Omissions Are Not Accidents: Gender in the Art of Marianne Moore* (Wayne State U Press), and the forthcoming collection of essays, co-edited with Tyrone Williams, *Inciting Poetics: Thinking and Writing Poetry* (U of New Mexico Press). Heuving is a professor in the Interdisciplinary Arts and Science program at the University of Washington (UW) Bothell and is on the graduate faculty in the English Department at UW Seattle. She is the recipient of grants from the Fulbright Foundation, National Endowment for the Humanities, Simpson Humanities Center, and the Beinecke Library at Yale.

Leslie Kaplan est née à New York en 1943, elle a été élevée à Paris dans une famille américaine, elle écrit en français. Après des études de philosophie, d'histoire et de psychologie, elle travaille deux ans en usine et participe au mouvement de Mai 68.
Son premier livre, *L'Excès-l'usine*, salué par Maurice Blanchot et Marguerite Duras, a été publié en 1982. Son oeuvre, publiée aux Editions POL et traduite dans une dizaine de langues, comprend des récits et des romans (notamment *Le livre des ciels, Le Criminel,*

Le pont de Brooklyn, Depuis maintenant-Miss Nobody Knows, Le Psychanalyste, Fever, Millefeuille, Mathias et la Révolution...), une autobiographie fragmentaire (*Mon Amérique commence en Pologne*), des essais (*Les Outils* et le site internet lesliekaplan.net), des pièces de théâtre (*Toute ma vie j'ai été une femme, Louise, elle est folle, Déplace le ciel*). Leslie Kaplan est membre du conseil de la revue Trafic. Elle a reçu le Prix Wepler pour le roman *Millefeuille* en 2012. En juin 2017 la Société des Gens de Lettres lui a attribué le Grand prix de la SGDL pour l'ensemble de son œuvre.

Stacey Levine has written four books of fiction: *The Girl with Brown Fur: Tales and Stories, Frances Johnson* (a novel), *Dra---* (a novel), and *My Horse and Other Stories*. A recipient of a PEN/West Fiction award and a Stranger Genius award for literature, she is working on MICE, a novel.

Sarah Mangold is the author of *Giraffes of Devotion* (Kore), *Electrical Theories of Femininity* (Black Radish), and *Household Mechanics* (New Issues). She is the recipient of a 2013 NEA Literature Fellowship and lives near Seattle.

Geraldine Monk's latest collection of poems *They Who Saw the Deep* was published in the USA by Free Verse Editions/Parlor Press in 2016. Her *The Three Stepping Stones of Dawn* was her most recent commission from *The Verb* on BBC Radio Three. She is an affiliated poet at the Centre for Poetry and Poetics, Sheffield University.

John Olson is the author of numerous books of prose poetry, including *Dada Budapest, Larynx Galaxy,* and *Backscatter: New and Selected Poems*. He has also authored four novels, including *In Advance of the Broken Justy, The Seeing Machine, The Nothing That Is,* and *Souls of Wind*, the latter of which was shortlisted for a *Believer Magazine* award in 2008. In 2004 the popular Seattle weekly, *The Stranger*, awarded him the Genius Award for literature.

Roberta Olson's work has appeared in numerous journals including Talisman, New American Writing, and Facture. Her work was also included in the Anthology "As If It Fell From the Sun, Ten Years of

Women's Writing" (EtherDome Press 2012). She is the author of two chapbooks "All These Fair and Flagrant Things" (EtherDome Press, 2001) and "Some Numerous Dwarf Rippings", Flash+Card Press, 2007. She lives in Seattle.

Mary Ann Peters makes paintings, drawings and installations and has received numerous awards for her work, including the Art Matters/Camargo Foundation 2016 fellowship for research in Marseille, France, the 2015 Stranger Genius Award in Visual Art, the 2010 MacDowell Colony Pollock/Krasner fellowship, and the 2000 Neddy Award in Painting. She is represented by the James Harris Gallery, Seattle, Washington.

Meredith Quartermain's most recent books are *U Girl: a novel* and *I, Bartleby: short stories* (both from Talonbooks, 2016 and 2015). Her *Vancouver Walking* (NeWest, 2005) won a BC Book Award for Poetry, and *Nightmarker* (NeWest, 2008) was a finalist for a Vancouver Book Award. She was Poetry Mentor at the SFU Writer's Studio from 2014-2016.

Marthe Reed's sixth collection, *ARK HIVE*, will be published by The Operating System (2019). Her poetry has been published in *BAX2014, New American Writing, Golden Handcuffs Review, Entropy, New Orleans Review, Jacket@, Fairy Tale Review, The Volta*, and *The Offending Adam*, among others. *Counter-Desecration: A Glossary for Writing in the Anthropocene*, co-edited with Linda Russo, will be published by Wesleyan University Press in 2018. Reed was co-publisher and managing editor for Black Radish Books; she lived in Syracuse, NY.

Joanna Ruocco is the author of several books, including, most recently, *Dan, The Week*, and *Field Glass*, written with Joanna Howard. She is an assistant professor in the English Department at Wake Forest University.

Lisa Samuels is a transnational poet whose recent books are *Tender Girl* (2015), *A TransPacific Poetics* (2017, anthology with co-editor Sawako Nakayasu), *Symphony for Human Transport* (2017), and *Foreign Native* (2018). She also writes essays and works with sound and film, including *Tomorrowland* (2017, directed by Wes Tank), based on her book & CDs. "Our lady of errata" is excerpted from a developing work, *The Long White Cloud of Unknowing*. Lisa lives in New Zealand and teaches at the University of Auckland.

Susan M. Schultz is author of two volumes of _Dementia Blog_ from Singing Horse Press and several volumes of _Memory Cards_,most recently the *Thomas Traherne series* from Talisman and the *Simone Weil* series from Equipage (UK). She is publisher and editor of Tinfish Press and lives in Kane'ohe, Hawai'i with her family. She is a lifelong fan of the St. Louis Cardinals.

Anne Tardos, French-born American poet, is the author of ten books of poetry and several performance works. Her writing is renowned for its fluid use of multiple languages and its innovative forms. Among her recent books of poetry are *The Camel's Pedestal, I Am You* [two editions], *NINE; Both Poems,* and *The Dik-dik's Solitude*. She is also the editor of three posthumous books of poetry by Jackson Mac Low, *Thing of Beauty, 154 Forties,* and *The Complete Light Poems* [with Michael O'Driscoll]. A Fellow in Poetry from the New York Foundation for the Arts, Tardos lives in New York.

Rosmarie Waldrop's most recent books are *Gap Gardening: Selected Poems*, and *Driven to Abstraction* (New Directions). Her novels, *The Hanky of Pippin's Daughter* and *A Form/of Taking/It All*, are available in one volume from Northwestern UP; her collected essays, *Dissonance (if you are interested)*, from U of Alabama Press. She has translated 14 volumes of Edmond Jabès's work (her memoir, *Lavish Absence: Recalling and Rereading Edmond Jabès*, is out from Wesleyan UP) as well as volumes by Emmanuel Hocquard, Jacques Roubaud, and, from the German, Friederike Mayröcker, Elke Erb, Peter Waterhouse, Gerhard Rühm. She lives in Providence, RI, where, with Keith Waldrop, she edited Burning Deck Press.

Catherine Walsh was born in Dublin, Ireland, in 1964, has spent some time living and working abroad, and currently lives in Limerick. She co-edits hardPressed Poetry with Billy Mills. Her chapbooks in print include: *Macula* (Red Wheelbarrow Press, Dublin: 1986); *The Ca Pater Pillar Thing and More Besides* (hardPressed Poetry, Dublin,

1986); *Making Tents* (hardPressed Poetry, Dublin, 1987); *Short Stories* (North & South, Twickenham and Wakefield, 1989); *Pitch* (Pig Press, Durham, 1994); *Idir Eatortha & Making Tents* (Invisible Books, London, 1996); *City West* (Shearsman, Exeter, 2005); *Optic Verve A Commentary* (Shearsman, Exeter, 2009); *Astonished Birds; Carla, Jane, Bob and James* (hardPressed Poetry, Limerick 2012).

Her work is included in a number of anthologies, including the *Anthology of Twentieth-Century British & Irish Poetry* (Oxford University Press, New York and Oxford, 2001) and *No Soy Tu Musa* (Ediciones Torremozas, Madrid, 2008), a bilingual Spanish/English anthology of Irish women poets.

She was Holloway Lecturer on the Practice of Poetry at the University of California, Berkeley for 2012/13 and was a research fellow with the Digital Humanities cluster at An Foras Feasa, Maynooth University during 2014/2015. Sections of *Barbaric Tales* have previously appeared in the spring/summer 2016 edition of the Irish University Review and in Uimhir a Cúig, Numero Cinq Vol. VII No. 10 October 2016. *The Beautiful Untogether* is initially available online thanks to Smithereens Press, Ireland.

The essential David Bromige

if wants to be the same as is

Essential Poems of David Bromige

Edited by Jack Krick, Bob Perelman, and Ron Silliman
With an introduction by George Bowering

'Among the three or four most significant writers of his generation.'

— Michael Davidson

"a poet of enormous intellect, humor and innovation who is always shifting out from under the solutions of the last book and posing new questions and linguistic possibilities for a song.'

—Kathleen Fraser

Publication date: June 21, 2018
Available through Small Press Distribution

www.newstarbooks.com

CPSIA information can be obtained
at www.ICGtesting.com
Printed in the USA
FFOW01n1000280518
46858221-49070FF